KING OF NEW YORK 3

Lock Down Publications and Ca$h
Presents
KING OF NEW YORK 3
A Novel by *T.J. EDWARDS*

Lock Down Publications
P.O. Box 870494
Mesquite, Tx 75187

Visit our website @
www.lockdownpublications.com

Copyright 2018 KING OF NEW YORK 3

First Edition March 2019
Printed in the United States of America

Lock Down Publications
Like our page on Facebook: Lock Down Publications
@
www.facebook.com/lockdownpublications.ldp
Cover design and layout by: **Dynasty Cover Me**
Book interior design by: **Shawn Walker**
Edited by: **Tisha Andrews**

Stay Connected with Us!

Text **LOCKDOWN** to 22828 to stay up-to-date with new releases, sneak peaks, contests and more…

Thank you.

Submission Guideline.

Submit the first three chapters of your completed manuscript to ldpsubmissions@gmail.com, subject line: Your book's title. The manuscript must be in a .doc file and sent as an attachment. Document should be in Times New Roman, double spaced and in size 12 font. Also, provide your synopsis and full contact information. If sending multiple submissions, they must each be in a separate email.

Have a story but no way to send it electronically? You can still submit to LDP/Ca$h Presents. Send in the first three chapters, written or typed, of your completed manuscript to:

LDP: Submissions Dept
Po Box 870494
Mesquite, Tx 75187

DO NOT send original manuscript. Must be a duplicate.

Provide your synopsis and a cover letter containing your full contact information.

Thanks for considering LDP and Ca$h Presents.

T.J. Edwards

Chapter 1
Showbiz

Six degrees below zero with the wind blowing a consistent eight miles an hour into my face, snow fell in thick patches from the night's sky. The sound of the L-Train screeched loudly on the tracks over my head. I balled my fingers into fists and blew into the palms of my gloves, creating some sort of relief for my frozen fingers. My black on black Bomber jacket was doing very little to protect me from the attack of the harsh winter.

I had on two pairs of thermal tops and bottoms with an extra pair of socks on my feet. I stomped my right foot two times, trying to get some sort of feeling into my foot. I'd been standing outside for a full hour waiting on my best friend, Evelina, to come back out of her father's store so we could take care of business.

Evelina and I had been best friends ever since the fourth grade where, back then, she'd been my girlfriend. It wasn't until we'd gotten into the tenth grade that she discovered her thirst for female flesh and decided to cast men to the side for the most part. By that time though, we'd become just good friends. It was after I'd developed a hunger for dating and screwing multiple women on a regular occasion.

Evelina saw the hoe in me and thought it wise for us to leave the dating aspect of our relationship behind. So, around the tenth grade, we started to flip bitches together and it had been on and popping ever since.

Evelina was 5'5" and caramel skinned. She was Jamaican and Puerto Rican. She had real long, curly hair that fell to her waist and light brown eyes like myself. She was born and raised in Spanish Harlem. And even though she was a female, she had more heart than any nigga I knew or had ever known. There was no one I trusted more than her to have my back when the heat was on.

My father and mother are both Cuban, born and raised in Havana. I, like Evelina, was born in Spanish Harlem, raised in the Dyckman Houses. They were low rent project buildings located in upper Manhattan, right off of Nagle and Tenth Avenue. At 6'1", weighing 180 pounds, I'd gotten my brown skin and light brown eyes from my father's side of the family. I kept my jet black, silky hair in a pony tail and was extremely fit. I've been in and out of the juvenile system my whole life. While on the inside, I developed a hunger for working out and keeping my body in shape.

I blew into my gloved hands one more time and looked up and down the alley I was waiting inside of. There were two big cats feasting on the discarded remains of a dead pitbull that had lost a fight only a few hours earlier up the street on Eleventh Avenue. Large portions of the dog was already covered by snow. There was also a pool of frozen blood that formed under its body. As the cats continued to gnaw at him, I could smell the stench of it from afar.

I heard a bunch of footsteps on the stairs inside of the store, the big wooden door swinging open to reveal Evelina standing behind it. She had a big smile on her face as she stepped into the back alley beside me with a duffle bag on her right shoulder. She kneeled down on one knee in front of me. She had a purple Fendi scarf around her neck I'd gotten her for our seventeenth birthday, a black skullcap on her head, and a big black Bomber jacket over her upper torso. She began to unzip the bag.

"Yo, that's my fault for taking so long, Showbiz. My old man was giving me the business in there. I had to wait until he went in the basement before I could grab these jokers. Here." She handed me a .40 Glock and then the clip to put inside of it.

The gun was all black with black tape around the handle. I slammed the clip into the bottom of it and cocked the gun before putting it on my waist. I tucked it into my waistband and pulled my jacket over it. "Why he put the tape on the handle of it?" I asked as the snow began to fall even harder from the sky. The wind picked up its speed and caused me to shiver. I felt like I was freezing.

She took another .40 Glock and slammed a clip into the bottom of it. She cocked it back and put it into the small of her back. She shrugged and wiped snow out of her face. "I don't know why he do half the shit he do. We gotta hurry up and bust this move though. I don't want to hear his mouth if he sees these pistols are missing."

I waved her to follow me. "Come on then."

We started to jog down the alley, past the big cats that were still gnawing away at the dead dog. I saw there were about ten alley rats taking bites out of the pitbull's flesh. There was a light in the alley that flashed on and off. I kept my jog to a nice even pace so I wouldn't leave Evelina behind. Most times when we would hit licks and had to run away, she had a hard time keeping up with me. More than a few times, I'd leave her in the dust and whenever we met up later that night, she'd always lose her mind. We'd wind up fighting like enemies. Therefore, I'd learned my lesson. I wasn't trying to go there with her tonight.

We hit it up the long flight of stairs and waited on the platform for the L-Train to come through. It was only ten o'clock at night and the platform, with the exception of us, was empty.

"Yo, you sure it's gon' be at least two kilos in there though?" I asked, getting excited.

I already knew how I was going to break down mine. I was gon' post up in the projects with straight nickel bags and push them jokers until I ain't have nothing left. Once I got my bread right, then I was gon' get up with my uncle Javier. He was the birdman and moved weight all the way from Havana to back home in New York. He was all about his paper. A supreme hustler. I wanted to eat in the same fashion as him and nobody was gonna tell me that I wasn't.

Evelina shivered and blew into her gloved hands. "I'm sure it's at least that in there. Damn, fool. How many times are you going to ask me that question?" She frowned and shook her head.

"As many times as I feel like it. I need some type of motivation to go in here and bust this nigga's ass. You know me and your brother kind of cool, Evelina. If he find out that we hitting his right hand man, you know it's gon' be some shit in the air between us." I rubbed my gloves together and looked down the train tracks to see if I could locate the L-Train. I got irritated because it was nowhere in sight.

"Charlie will be alright. He knows that this shit is a part of the game. Max shouldn't be so damn flashy. He be acting like he want his stuff to get taken, so we might as well get it before anybody else. And for the record, it's at least two kilos in there. When I was over there last night with Charlie, I'd seen at least four. That fool ain't sold that merch that fast. At least I don't think so." She looked down the railroad tracks for the train, as well. "Hey, Showbiz. You know I don't like it when you call me by my full name, so knock that shit off before I start to calling you Juanito," she said and snickered.

Juanito was my first name and I hated it. My father who'd basically named me after my mother, Juanita, gave the name to me. I'd named myself Showbiz and the name had stuck with me. I was a real flashy type nigga. I had to have the best of the best, even when I couldn't afford it. I knew that someday I would strike it big. Then the name Showbiz would have its full effect. I couldn't see myself being in the hood forever hitting licks and struggling to make ends meet. I was destined to be a king. It was in my blood and in my heart.

"A'ight, Eve. That's my bad. I just like fucking with you from time to time, that's all." I nudged her shoulder.

She smiled and shook her head. "Yeah, well don't, nigga. That name makes me miss my mother. Remember, she's the one that gave it to me. Every time I hear you say it, I think about how she looked lying in that hospital, struggling for her last breath after my grandfather had beaten her head in." She sighed and dropped her chin to her chest. "I miss my mother so much, Showbiz. I wonder if she's still looking down on me."

I put my arm around her shoulder and pulled her into my embrace, kissing her on the cheek. "Of course, she is. I bet she was looking down on us when we put them slugs in your grandfather after he got out of the county jail too, huh?" I joked.

She elbowed me in the ribs. "Shut up. You always gotta say the craziest shit."

Eve watched her grandfather beat her mother senseless when she was just a young teen of sixteen years old. Her mother had been struggling with a heroin addiction for many years. One night she'd been feening for the drug and decided to steal a fifty-dollar bill from Eve's grandfather, but she was caught in the process.

Eve's grandfather beat her mother over the head with a billy club until she was unconscious. He then called the police and told them what happened. Eve's mother was taken to the hospital where she died two days later from internal bleeding of the brain. It was a sad day in both our lives.

A day after her mother passed on, her grandfather was arrested for the murder. He'd bailout the next day and two days after that, she and I gunned him down in the back of the local bar that he frequented. I felt the murder helped Eve cope with the situation. After we'd killed her grandfather, she'd seemed more brighter, more alive. That was until her mother's name was brought up at any given time. Then she'd become silent and seem depressed.

The platform began to rumble. I could hear the screeching of the L-Train fast approaching.

Eve pushed me away from her and put a mug on her face. "Enough of that lovey dovey shit, nigga. Let's go and handle this business."

* * *

By the time we made it to Max's house, the snow was coming down so hard, the city looked like a plain white, blank sheet of paper. On top of that, the wind increased by at least five miles. It was blowing so hard, I was struggling to keep my ground. Eve stepped up to the door of the brownstone and knocked on the door with her knuckles. As soon as she was stopped, she blew into her fists to warm them. I could tell she was cold because she was shaking like a leaf.

Max stayed in the Harlem River Houses on West 152nd and 7th Avenue. I'd been around the area a few times whenever I kicked it with her older brother, Charlie. I really didn't like the area because it was so grimy. Most of the niggas there were Crips and they were super gang bangers. I didn't really get along with too many Crip niggas because I'd grown up around nothing but Bloods and cold-hearted Latin Kings. The Crips were on the other side of Spanish Harlem across the Harlem River Park. I ain't fuck with that area.

Max answered the door two minutes later with bloodshot eyes and a bottle of Hornitos in his hand with the cap off. He looked from Eve then to me and hiccupped. "What the fuck y'all doing here?" he asked, licking his dry lips.

13

Eve brushed past him and I did the same thing. We made our way up the stairs in silence. I looked behind me to see him close the door at the bottom of the flight and lock it. I curled my lip as I felt the beats of my heart speed up.

When I stepped through the door of his crib, it smelled like heavy Primos. Primos were weed-filled cigars mixed with crack cocaine. Max and Charlie were known for smoking these things. I hated being around them when they did because they smelled so fucking bad. It nearly blew my mind when I saw Charlie sitting at living room table with a razor blade in his hand, chopping through about a half ounce of cocaine. He looked up with glossy eyes and wiped his mouth. He was shirtless and shoeless.

Eve bucked her eyes and looked up to me. "Damn, this nigga's here." She walked over to him with a mug on her face. "What are you doing here, Charlie? Damn, I thought you had to work tonight."

He grunted, "Bitch, why you worried about where I am or what I'm doing? I'm grown as a mutha-fucka, so mind yo' business." Charlie was a heavyset nigga. He was 5'7" and weighed about 280 pounds. He was tatted up with all of that Crip shit on him. He was her half-brother, full-blooded Jamaican on her father's side.

Eve slammed her hand on the table. "Nigga, I done told you about calling me out of my fucking name. Do it again and we about to tear this bitch up," she snapped.

I slid my hand under my shirt. I knew Charlie was her brother and everything, but Eve was my right hand. If that nigga thought he was about to put his hands on her, I was finna light his ass up and we still was going to rob Max's ass blind. I was already one of them real trigger-happy niggas anyway. I didn't give a fuck about smoking him or Max. I'm just being honest.

Max stepped past me and locked the upstairs door. "Damn, why every time you two muthafuckas get together, y'all are always at each other's throats? Damn. A muhfucka ain't trying to hear all that noise today. Shut up!" He bumped Eve out of the way and pulled the chair out she'd been standing in front of.

"Excuse you, Max. Fuck!" Eve hollered, looking down on him with a scowl on her face.

He ignored her and pulled the mirror the pile of cocaine was on, chopping through it with a razor blade. "What brings you two over to my crib anyway?" he asked, looking up at her with a smirk on his face. " I know y'all ain't copping shit." He laughed at his own joke.

I noticed more than a few big roaches crawling over his stained walls. There was one crawling on top of the ceiling that looked as if it were going to drop at any minute. It had a roach egg hanging out of the back of it. His carpet was filthy.

Once white, it now took on the color of gray. The furniture looked worn. The television's volume appeared to be all the way up, blasting a commercial. There were shoes everywhere and it was so hot that I could barely breathe. I could feel my skin sweating against the cool steel of the .40 Glock.

Eve looked down on him. "For your information, we came to see what kind of a deal you'd give us on a few ounces of dog food. I figured you'd look out since you holding now." She looked up at me with an evil look in her eyes.

Max looked over his shoulder at her. "Bitch, you ain't giving me no pussy. What the fuck I look like giving you any type of deal when ain't no benefits to it? You got me fucked up."

He grabbed the bottle of Hornitos off of the table and turned it up. Max was about 5'11", a dark-skinned Jamaican with brown eyes. He was born and raised in Harlem. He was a real skinny nigga because he did a lot of dope over the years.

"Say, son. Watch that bitch word when you referring to her. We come over here to put some money in yo' pocket, not for all this other shit," I said, feeling the beats of my heart thumping in my chest.

Like I said before, Eve and I had been a part of each other ever since the fourth grade. Over the years, we'd grown incredibly close. I had her back and she had mine. Didn't no bitches disrespect me and get away with it if she was around and wasn't no nigga about to get at her disrespectfully in my presence. I knew she could hold her own, but I rarely gave her the chance to.

"N'all, it's good, Showbiz. You ain't gotta say nothing to this punk ass nigga. He only doing what he see my brother doing to me. And that's fucked up, Charlie."

"Yo, that shit ain't got nothing to do with me. My mans say he ain't giving you no deals, so that's what it is. Far as what he called you, you are a female, right? I mean just because you fuck with bitches don't mean you ain't one. They say you are what you eat, so…" He laughed to himself and Max joined in.

Eve sucked her teeth and nodded. "A'ight, so if that's how y'all wanna play shit then it's good. I ain't gon' sweat it. Max, me and Showbiz wanna cop a bird of heroin, so what's good?"

Charlie scrunched his face and looked over to me and then her. "We ain't fucking with this Blood nigga like that. Only reason I ain't been put two in his head is 'cause you fuck with him, but it ain't going down like that. We don't accept Blood money. That's what it is," Charlie spat, mugging me with hatred.

"And I don't sell dope to bitches anyway. So, even if ya' mans wasn't a fucking Tampon, I wouldn't give you a gram of heroin up out this bitch. That's my word."

"That's yo' word, huh?" I asked, feeling my blood boiling inside of me. I was on the verge of losing my head.

"Yeah, fuck boy. That's my word," Max retorted.

Eve upped her .40 Glock out of the small of her back and smacked him across the face with it so hard, it went off.

Boom!

T.J. Edwards

Chapter 2

The gun spat fire in her hand as it made contact with Max's face, sending him off of the chair with a big split in his forehead. Eve's bullet flew into Charlie's shoulder. He grabbed it as blood oozed through his fingers and dripped off his wrist.

"Aw, fuck, Eve. What did you do?" he growled in agony.

"I told you, fuck nigga, about calling me out of my name. Y'all gon' respect me. That's on everything I love!" she hollered.

I jumped into action, grabbed Max by his pony-tail and stuck my Glock into his cheek. "Nigga, where dem chickens at? I know they here and if you make me work to get 'em, I'm smoking you. That's on my blood, nigga."

I pulled him away from the table aggressively and planted my Timbs on his chest. I cocked the hammer of the Glock, ready to punch a hole in his face. I didn't like how he'd came at Eve or disrespected my Blood niggas. I was thinking I was gon' bag his ass whether he complied with my demands or not.

Charlie fell out of his chair and onto the carpet with blood skeeting out of the big hole in his shoulder. "Eve, what the fuck are you doing? I know you ain't about to rob me with this nigga? I'm yo' fucking brother."

Eve rushed over to him and slapped him across the face with her gun. His head crashed into the wall he was laying against. "You just my half-brother, nigga. Showbiz more of my brother than you'll ever be!" She smacked him again and then grabbed a handful of his collar, placing the gun to his forehead. "Where is the dope, Charlie? Please don't make us do this shit to you. I am begging you. We ain't leaving this bitch until we got everything that we've come for."

I choked Max for a good thirty seconds, then put the barrel of my gun against the middle of his forehead. "I ain't gon' ask you again, my nigga."

Max nodded. "A'ight, man. Damn, it's in my bedroom in the dresser. It's five kilos, man. Y'all take that shit and just leave."

"Eve, go check and make sure this nigga ain't lying. I'll keep watch. Hurry up," I ordered, dragging Max by the collar of his shirt and dropping him next to Charlie.

Eve jumped up and nodded. She looked down on Charlie and frowned. "If his bitch ass move, you put a slug in him. It's no mercy for these fuck niggas. They ain't got no love or respect for us, so we ain't got none for them. It is what it is. That's my word." She ran out of the living room toward the back of the house where Max's bedroom was located.

"Y'all ain't gon' get away with this, son. You muthafuckas think y'all gon' rob my mans and ain't shit gon' happen. Yeah, the fuck right. My sister's a dead nigga just like you. I'ma make sure of that," Charlie promised with blood leaking from the tear in his lip.

Max struggled to put his back against the wall. "It's good, son. You already know what it is. Both of them dead, kid. Word is bond." He spat blood onto the carpet and wiped his mouth, looking up at me.

I kicked him in the chest with so much force, it knocked the wind out of him. He ended up on his side, gasping for air. I leaned over and punched Charlie in the jaw, rocking his ass. His head snapped violently to the right before he passed out. "Both of you soft ass niggas shut the fuck up! Ain't nobody gon' touch Eve or the god. Get that shit through ya wigs right now." I kicked Max in the ribs, propping his ass upward.

Eve walked into the living room and dropped a black plastic bag on the floor. "Yo, Showbiz. This fuck nigga tried to hold out. He had birds all in the mattress, son. I got all of them shits. It's ten total. We good to go."

After hearing the amount of product we'd come up on, I got excited. Ten birds in Harlem would make us a pretty penny, especially on how I was planning to handle business. "Yo, that's what's good. What we finna do with them, though?" I was ready to send both of them niggas to the reaper. I lived by the rules of never allowing a man to walk away with his life after I'd pulled a gun out on him. I knew Charlie was her brother but in this scenario, I felt he was a casualty of war. He had to go. I was praying that she saw shit my way.

She stepped up to Max and extended her gun. "Fuck you mean what we gon' do with them? We gon' do with them like we do with everybody else that cross our paths on some fuck shit. These niggas gotta go. Both of 'em."

Max lifted his head and before she could react, he lunged at her and grabbed a hold of the gun. I aimed and fired two shots directly at his head. The first one slammed into the wall. The second one crashed into his neck and created a big hole that leaked profusely. He twisted in the air before landing on top of the table with his arms out stretched. A puff of cocaine wafted into the air in a big cloud.

Eve jumped back and aimed her gun at him, squeezing the trigger twice, sending her bullets into his back. He jerked on the table and fell to the floor. "Bitch ass nigga tried to go on me, huh, Blood?"

Charlie shook his head and came out of his dazed state. He placed his hand on the wall and struggled to make it to his feet with blood streaming down the side of his mouth.

"Yo, Eve. Let me smoke this nigga, ma. You know we can't leave him alive, so am I killing him or are you gon' do it?" I asked, aiming my pistol at him ready to blow his shit all over the wall. In my mind, he had to go. I needed to leave that house knowing that this fuck nigga was on his way to the morgue.

Eve raised her gun and aimed at him with her eyes lowered. "N'all, I got this, Showbiz. If anybody gon' send this fool on his way, it's gon' be me. It's only right, nah'mean?"

Charlie placed his back against the wall and held his hands out in front of him. "Come on, Eve. You ain't gotta do this shit. Please, lil' sis. I swear to God I won't say nothing. I ain't coming for y'all. Just go!" he shouted. He wrapped his arm around his ribs and doubled over, breathing loudly.

Eve shook her head. "N'all, Charlie. I can't do that. You gotta take the heat with ya mans, son. Plus, I told you that one day I'd get yo' ass back for every-thing you did to me as a little girl. Now it's time to pay the piper, nigga. Take this shit like a man." She bit into her lower lip, ready to buck at him.

He held his hands up further. "Wait, wait, wait! Please, think about Tasha. Who gon' take care of her? I'm the only provider she got. You know her mother ain't on shit. At least let me live for her."

Tasha was Charlie's ten-year-old daughter. She was Eve's favorite niece. Most of the time after she and I hit a lick, she would made sure she spent some of the money on Tasha. She'd always told me she felt Charlie was a bit of a dead beat—he cared more about putting dope up his nose than taking care of his little girl. Tasha's mother was just as bad and every bit of a dope head that Charlie was. Tasha had been born to two trifling ass parents. Eve felt sorry for her and did all that she could.

Eve looked him over for a long time, then she slowly began to lower her pistol. "I don't know if I can trust you, Charlie. Who's to say that you won't rat us out to the cops if we let you go?" she asked him this time looking up to me.

Charlie shook his head. "You know I don't fuck with the law like that. I'd rather die than go to the police." He exhaled loudly, and sank to his ass. "We slipped up. We gotta take this shit on the chin. It is what it is." He wrapped his arms around his legs in submission. Roaches crawled on the wall behind him.

Eve lowered her gun all the way and sighed. "Let's go, Showbiz. That nigga ain't gon' tell on us. I know him better than that."

I jerked my head back. I was flabbergasted. "What? You think I'm about to let this nigga live?

You got me fucked up." I threw the table to the side. As soon as I did, Charlie jumped up and took off running down the hall. I aimed and squeezed the trigger twice, sending a slug into his back. He flew forward and landed in a push up position with blood squirting out of the hole in his back. He struggled to get up.

"Showbiz, fuck it. Kill that nigga. Hurry up, I think I hear sirens." She picked up the bag of dope and opened the back door.

I rushed down the hall. "Turn over, Blood."

He coughed and slowly turned on to his back. "Fuck you, Showbiz. You gon' get yours one day, B. Word is bond. Fuck you!" He spit blood at me.

I stood over him and smoked my gun three times. All facials. Splattering him on the carpet. I looked into his wide eyes and felt giddy. I'd never really liked Charlie's fat ass. He was way too cocky and disrespectful for me.

"Showbiz, nigga bring ya ass on!" Eve hollered in Spanish.

Seconds later, we were running down the back steps and out of the brownstone.

* * *

Eve started pacing in front of me. We were sitting in the basement of my crib when she'd jumped up and started. All ten of the kilos were on the table in front of me wrapped in aluminum foil and plastic. "I know his death finna fuck with me, Showbiz. After my mom died, I saw her every single day in my dreams for a year straight. That drove me crazy. " She ran her fingers through her curly hair and sighed out

24

loud. She'd taken off her blouse, wearing her red lace bra.

"Eve, I get it, but fuck that nigga. Think about all of the shit he did to you when you were a little kid. We always said that we'd smoke his ass one day. Now it's done. Fuck it, let's move on with life. Nah'mean?"

I took my pocket knife and sliced down the edge of one of the kilos, pulling the plastic off it, then a portion of the aluminum foil. After breaking off a chunk, I sat it on the small saucer in front of me and crumbled the product into dust. It looked snow white. I knew I was looking at pristine China White. I could feel it tingling my fingers.

Eve's eyes got watery. She shook her head and sighed out loud again. "I hated every time he touched me, Showbiz. I swear to God I did. He took more advantage of me than anybody who ever came across my path." She lowered her head. "But he was still my father's son and because of me, he is no longer breathing."

I took a small portion of the heroin and put it on to the tip of my finger. I sniffed it up my right nostril and waited for the effects of the drug to take over me. It didn't take long. In just a few seconds, I was floating on air. My body felt numb. There was a sudden case of intense euphoria that swept over me. I was so happy, I could barely think straight.

Suddenly, I couldn't understand why Eve was so mad or broken up about the death of Charlie. He'd been molesting her every since she was eight years old and he was twenty. I could recall numerous nights where she'd sneak out of her house to come and sleep in the bed with me. I held her the whole night through after he'd taken advantage of her in many unimaginable ways. I wanted to kill him a long time ago.

"Yo, it ain't your fault, ma. I smoked his punk ass and if I had to, I'd do it again. That punk wasn't your brother, he was your abuser. He met that steel. Let his bitch ass rest in hell for all I care. Come here." I patted the spot on the couch next to me and scooted over a lil' bit.

She waved me off. "N'all, I ain't ready to sit down just yet. I gotta pace so I can get this feeling out of my system. What that dope taste like?" she asked, looking down at it.

"It's good. Here. Come get you a taste." I placed a lil' bit on the table and made two quick lines for her.

She took a twenty dollar bill out of her Jordache jean pocket and rolled it into a straw. She sat on the couch and lowered her head, tooting the lines with expertise. After she finished, she held her nose and sat back on the couch with her eyes closed. "Yeah, that's it right there. Fuck that's good."

I made me two thin lines and followed suit. Once I really felt the dope pumping through my body, I laid back with a smile on my face. I felt like I was floating on Aladdin's carpet. There was a soothing jazz-like music playing in my head. I could feel my entire body vibrating. My dick was hard as ever and I felt free as a bird.

Eve stood up and pulled her jeans down her thick thighs. Under them she had on a pair of red lace boy shorts that looked a size too small for her. She pulled them all the way up into her crease and then kneeled in front of me, pulling my Polos off of my ankles. Once they were off, she turned around and sat on my lap, trapping my dick head with her ass cheeks. "Mmm, you like how that feel, Showbiz?" She laid her back on my chest and rotated her ass in a slow, circular motion.

I pulled her into my embrace and rubbed all over her thick thighs. My face was in the crux of her neck, sniffing at her Vibe perfume. "You know I love when you get up here, but I already know you on some tease me shit. You ain't trying to let me hit this pussy tonight, are you?" I slid my fingers into her waist band and rubbed all over her naked cat lips. They were puffy and heavily engorged. A slight trace of her essence was on the lips. The gel was slippery and felt rich.

She opened her thighs wider as I located her clitoris, trapping it between my fingers. "Uh, Showbiz." She bucked on my lap and massaged my dick with her ass. "You don't know what I'm in the mood to do tonight. I need to take my mind off of Charlie and it's only one way to do that. Plus, this dope got me feeling righteous." She turned her head to the side and licked along my face. Sucking my earlobe into her mouth, she began to moan.

I slid my middle finger into her oven. Her puffy lips wrapped around it and sucked me further in. Her big ass slid along my dick and pumped it. I could feel the heat from her naked skin and the material brushing against my meat. Both of them working together collectively drove me crazy. She smelled so good on top of everything else.

Even though Eve and I were just good friends and she fucked strictly with women, every now and then, she'd get into a mood where she needed to feel my dick beating down her walls. Those were the times I often looked forward to because her pussy was bomb. Tight, wet, and fit me just right.

Not to mention that she was a complete animal in the sack whenever we got right down to it. I leaned her all the way back and pushed her bra upward, taking her brown beauties and pushing them together. Both nipples were erect and appeared hungry for my mouth. I sucked the left one with my lips and pulled on it. She was twisted at an awkward angle to help me reach it.

"Wait, Showbiz. Let me turn around." She stood up and I caught a glimpse of her panties lodged deep within her crease. Both pussy lips appeared on either side of it. She slowly eased her way back down and straddled me. Taking her bra and throwing it to the floor, she wrapped her arms around my neck. "A'ight, nigga. Come on."

I grabbed them perfect titties and smushed them together, sucking on both nipples at the same time. They were hard against my lips.

"Aw, fuck, Showbiz. You got my pussy so wet. I think I need you to fuck me as hard as you can. I need that dick deep in this pussy, kid. Word up." She reached between her thighs and pulled her panties all the way to one side, exposing her meaty sex lips that had her vagina's cream all over them.

I stood up and flipped her on to her back on the couch, kneeled and pushed her knees to her chest before sucking her whole pussy into my mouth, slurping up the juices.

"Ah, fuck! Here you go. Ooh, shit." She took two fingers and opened her lips wide for me.

Her center looked like a wet rose. It was bubble gum pink. I licked up and down the slit and twirled my tongue around her clitoris before nipping at it with my teeth like I know she craved. I watched her peel her lips all the way back, busting that pussy wide open. I could smell the scent of her more clearly now. Pussy, with a hint of sweat and perfume. It was a concoction that had my dick jumping. I slid two fingers into her and worked them in and out as fast as I could go. At the same time, I sucked on her clit.

She wrapped her thick thighs around my head and humped into my face. "I'm gonna cum, Showbiz. I'm gonna cum! Aw, shit. Here I go, baby. Here I go! Fuck!" She threw her head back and bucked into my mouth. She was forcing my face further into her crease, riding my face for all it was worth.

Her juices ran down my neck and collarbone and I kept on eating and swallowing. Her thick ass rode my face while I squeezed my dick and pumped it in preparation of getting some of that ass. I needed some bad as hell.

She pushed me away and opened her thick thighs as wide as they could go. I watched her take two fingers and fuck herself, rolling her thumb around her clit in fast circles. "Let me see your dick, Showbiz. Come on. I need to see all of that meat." She whimpered and ran her tongue over her juicy lips.

I stood up naked, pumping my dick. The head looked as if it was ready to burst. "Here it go, Eve.

Look at this muhfucka. See how big it is?" I pulled the skin all the way back and held it at the base with my fist, resting on my balls.

"Hell yeah, I see. Bring it up here a lil' bit. I wanna put it in my mouth. Let me suck that big ass head." She opened her brown lips wider and continued to drive her fingers in and out of herself. Juices oozed out of her slit and slid down to her ass crack, wetting it. With her thighs spread so wide, I could see how her anus glistened in the light of the basement. It was highly arousing for me.

I straddled her body and fed her my dick. "Here, Eve. Handle yo' business." I closed my eyes as I felt her wrap her lips around my head and suck me into her mouth. I reached between her legs and played in her wet pussy. Opening her lips wider, I could feel her heat searing my hand as she humped up against it like a horny dog.

Gwk! Gwk! Gwk! Gwk! was the sound her mouth made as it slid up and down my pole. Her tongue would enter into the pee hole before she'd suck me all the way to my nut sack.

"Damn, Eve. I can't hold back. It's too good, ma. This head is too good. I'm finna cum in yo' mouth. You betta swallow this shit, too. Aww, you hear me?" I fucked into her mouth faster and faster as she tightened her lips to grip me better. My body got to tingling. My knees got weak. It felt like my spine was being peeled off of my back.

She continued to suck my dick as if it were a big ass straw. My eyes rolled into the back of my head. She sucked harder and harder and stroked me faster and faster with her little hand until it became too much. I tensed up and got to cumming all into her orifice. She continued to suck, swallowing my seed while she helped me to play in her pussy. Both of our fingers tried to work their way into her hole at the same time.

After cumming, I pulled out of her mouth and got on top of her body. I threw her thick thighs around me and rubbed my dick head up and down her slit. I was ready to slide into that pussy and beat her walls loose, but she put her hands on my chest before I could take that plunge.

"Wait, Showbiz. Let's not do this tonight, big homey. My mind ain't gon' be in it. Can you just hold me for a lil' while?" she asked, looking into my light brown eyes with her own.

On everything, I wanted to tell her, *Hell n'all. I wanna fuck this pussy, and hear you moaning that good shit all in my ear*. I wanted to push her knees to her chest and fuck her as hard as I could while I sucked all over her ankles and pretty toes, but the love I had for her prevailed. I sat back and nodded. "Yeah, I can do that, shorty. I know you going through some shit right now, and I'm here for you." I pulled her on top of my lap, and let her put her face in the crux of my neck while my dick rested against her wet pussy.

We ended the night just like that, with me holding her. She cried just a tad bit over Charlie's bitch ass, and I guess that was to be expected. For the remainder of the night, I just did and said whatever I had to in order to console her. I knew she needed me, and I felt it was my place to be there for her, even though all I really wanted to do was fuck that pussy until I passed out.

Chapter 3

I had a main bitch. Her name was Punkin. She was 5'6", caramel with brown eyes. She weighed about a 130 pounds. She was strapped. She had a flat stomach and a big ass, with some real double D breasts that had huge nipples on the ends on of them. Her hair was shoulder length, and for the most part, it was always permed or straightened. She was fashionista if I'd ever seen one. Shorty owned her own beauty salon and nail shop at the age of twenty years old. I found that admirable.

About three weeks after we'd robbed Max and Charlie for all of that heroin, I was in my crib aluminum foiling up a half kilo of dope. I was with two of my young Blood niggas when Punkin stepped into the crib with her sister, Tori. Tori was 5'4" with caramel skin and brown eyes. She was just as thick as Punkin, but she was slightly bow legged. Her hair was shaved on the sides, and she had this real cute curly mohawk-like thing going on. It was sexy and fit her to the tee in my opinion.

So, this day, I was just finishing up the half-kilo when Punkin came into the crib and dropped her Hermes bag on the couch. She was mugging everybody that sat in the kitchen getting my work together. That half-kilo was set to make me $75,000 in cash. They were bagged in all nickels so I wouldn't have to take no shorts. And because the dope was so good and pure, the feens were eating it up. I'd already popped two other kilos by this time and had a hundred and fifty bands put in the safe. I was almost ready to fuck with my uncle Javier out in Havana to get a major plug on the heroin and cocaine. I knew he'd hit me real nice if I could come up with at least a quarter of a million dollars. So that was my goal.

Punkin stepped into the kitchen and crossed her arms in front of her chest. "What the fuck is going on up in here? Didn't I tell you that my sister would be flying in from Gary, Indiana today, Showbiz? The least you could have done was have the house decent for her." She rolled her eyes and mugged my niggas.

I scoffed and dropped the last bit of dope in the aluminum foiled package that I was bagging up. Then I scooted away from the table and took my latex gloves off. I got up and grabbed her by her hair, taking her into the living room. "Punkin, I done told you about yo' slick ass mouth, right? Yet, you still keep pulling this fuck shit." I tossed her ass on the couch.

She yelped and bounced up from it, preparing to run at me. "I'm tired of this shit, Showbiz. You always putting your hands on me." She balled up her fists and closed her eyes, swinging wildly.

I took a step back and to the side before smacking her across the face so hard that she fell to the carpet, holding it with a stunned look on her face. "Bitch, you acting out 'cause of this audience. A'ight." I pulled off my Ferragamo belt, rolled it around my hand twice before grabbing a handful of her hair and whacking her across the ass with the belt five quick times.

She yelped each time and kicked her legs. "Let me go, Showbiz! Let me go! Don't do this shit in front of my sister. Please!" she begged, fighting against my hand that had taken ahold of her hair.

Tori backed against the wall with her hands over her face. "Oh my God. Oh my God, Punkin. Please, just shut up so he can be done!" she hollered.

I was tearing Punkin ass up with no remorse. Nothing irritated me as much as a female who didn't know how to stay in her own lane and the fuck out of mine. My mother had the same issue when I was growing up, and I'd watched my father nearly stomp a mud hole into her day in and day out. No matter how much he beat her ass, she never got the message it seemed because the next day she'd be popping off at the tongue all over again.

My mother had once told me that every woman needed to get their ass whooped from time to time. It kept them in line. When a man went too long of a period without getting into his woman's ass, it caused the power to shift in the relationship. A woman would then, more than likely, begin to test her man's masculinity. And no man should ever want for a woman to test him in that manner.

I gave her twenty more slashes across her ass and flung her to the floor. "Get yo' ass up and meet me in the room. Now!" I ordered. "And Tori, you sit yo' ass down. We'll be back out in a minute."

Tori sat on the couch and refused to make eye contact with me. She placed her Gucci bag on her lap and looked off into the distance. I could tell that she ain't want no smoke whatsoever.

Punkin slowly got up off the floor and made her way down the hallway with tears in her eyes. When she got to the bedroom, she plopped on the bed and crossed her thick legs. Her short skirt rode up and exposed her blue panties. "You didn't have to do me like that in front of her, Showbiz."

I closed the door and threw my belt on the bed. "I don't give a fuck about that bitch. She ain't mine. I'ma be who the fuck I am and that's all there is to it. If you ain't feeling it, you can pack yo' shit and get the fuck out. Word is bond."

Even though I cared about Punkin, she got on my nerves like a muthafucka. She was always saying something or doing something that grinded my gears. There had been so many times I had wanted to kick her ass to the curb but hadn't because I knew she was a good girl.

I'd been in and out of the county jail for three months at a time, and she'd held me down with no problem. She kept the phone on, money on my books, and made sure I stayed in contact with my Blood niggas in the slums. I felt like I owed her a since of loyalty on the one hand, but on the other I just wanted to muff her ass.

"Nigga, you love that. You think I'm finna leave so you can let some other bitch be all up in here laying in my place? You got me fucked up, nigga. I'd kill ya ass first. Don't get it twisted." She rolled her eyes, went into her bra, and pulled out a roll of hundreds, tossing it to me. "Here, with yo' ungrateful ass."

I caught the roll of cash, took the rubber band off of it, and started to count it. "How much is this?" I asked, thumbing through the money. I didn't give a fuck what total she told me, I was still going to count and make sure it was accurate.

She touched the corner of her mouth with her tongue and swallowed. "That's ten thousand. It's what the shop made in the last three days. I want you to put it with your stash so it can go toward the strip club you trying to open out in Harlem. You know I got your back, baby." She smiled and bit into her bottom lip.

That was another thing about Punkin. Every time she did one thing that pissed me off, she'd do something that would make me feel sorry for getting in her ass. Like I said before, I knew she was a good girl which is one of the reasons I kept her around.

It took me just a few minutes to confirm that she'd given me $10,000. I cuffed it and put it into my pocket. Grabbed her off of the bed and kissed her on the lips. "Good looking, boo. You know I appreciate you and couldn't do most of the shit I do without you standing by my side." I hugged her, bringing her body to mine and sucked on her neck.

She melted in my embrace and then pushed me away from her. "Showbiz, I'm not gon' keep letting you put your hands on me forever. One of these days, I'ma fight yo ass back and get the best of you. Mark my words on that." She wiped the small trace of blood from the corner of her mouth where I slapped the shit out of her. Seeing it made me feel some type of way. That was until my mother's words popped into my head.

"Yo, all you gotta do is respect my gangsta, and I wouldn't have to get all in your ass. One way or another, you gon' honor me because I'm the one making shit happen around this bitch. Right? Who's the one that makes sure both of our businesses stay up and running and you got all of the supplies you need, even when business has been a lil' slow, huh?"

She lowered her head. "You, daddy, and I've never said that you don't handle your business. You just have to keep your hands to yourself, that's all. I mean we have a good life together with the exception of that."

I slid my belt back into the loops of my pants. "Long as you fucking with me and you running that mouth, I'ma put yo' ass in check. That's how it's gotta go. It was like that for my pops and my mother and it's gon' be like that with me and any bitch I'm fucking with. I been like this since day one. Ain't no changing this gangsta, like it or love it."

Punkin shook her head and sighed. "Damn, you so lucky my whole life revolve around yo' ass. Then I just found out that I'm six weeks pregnant with your kid, so it looks like I'm locked in forever or at least the next eighteen years."

I was slipping my .45 into the small of my back when I'd heard the last part from her. My eyes got bucked. "What the fuck you mean you pregnant? When did you find this out?" I asked, walking in front of her. I didn't know if I was ready to be a father. I still had so many things that I wanted to accomplish before I brought a baby into the world. I wanted to at least have five million to my name before that happened. And that wasn't including assets. I was a certain type of nigga, always had been.

Punkin looked up at me. "Yeah, Showbiz. I'd missed my period all this month, so I got a lil' nervous and I took a home pregnancy test. It came back positive, but I didn't stop there. I took it one step further and went to the doctor. They confirmed that I was yesterday. I was gon' tell you over dinner or something tonight, but after seeing all that work in the kitchen, I can tell that you're going to be out all night busting moves. So, I'm telling you now."

I shook my head and sighed. "Yo, I don't even know if I'm ready for all of that right now. I'm still in these streets, ma. A kid ain't gon' do shit but slow me down and fuck up my groove. We gon' have to talk about this a lil' later to find out what we gon' do. A'ight?" I wiped the sweat from my forehead and on to my pants leg.

Punkin stood up and scrunched her face. "What is that supposed to mean? You're making it seem as if there is another option here when there isn't. It doesn't matter if you're ready or not, this baby is coming. You got eight more months to get your shit together, or else I'ma have to figure things out on my own. I'm resilient enough. I'd prefer for you to be beside me but if not, as a woman, I got this." She stepped into the bathroom that was connected to our room and slammed the door. "It's time to grow up, Showbiz. Grow the fuck up, right away."

An hour later, I was parked in the parking lot of the Dyckman Houses out in Spanish Harlem in an all-black Chevy Astro, popping nickel bags of heroin with Eve sitting in the passenger's seat.

"Damn, Showbiz. How the fuck you let her get pregnant though? Nigga, you know you ain't ready for no fucking kids. We beefing with all types of niggas out here." She adjusted the pistol on her lap and looked out of the passenger's window.

A male dope addict walked up to her side and stood in front of the glass. He danced from one foot unto the next. His lips were crusty white and so chapped, they were bleeding. He smelled like the strongest kind of funk and ass. He scratched at his neck and jerked his neck forward as if something was wrong with him. "Can—can I have a few of them nickel bags?" he asked, scratching at his forearm so hard that he left bloody streaks. There was snot drooling from is nose into his mouth.

Eve pinched her nose and frowned. "Damn, son. My word, you smell foul as hell. I shouldn't give you shit until you go and wash your stinky ass." She gagged.

I was so mad that this funky ass nigga's scent was coming into the car that I felt like getting out and whooping his ass. I mean I was furious as I pinched my nose. "Yo, Eve? Serve that fool so he can be on his way. Word is bond, he about to make me throw up that Taco Bell we just ate."

Eve reached in between her legs and dug into her bag. She grabbed five nickel bags and closed her fists around them. "Where the money at, nigga?"

The Hype looked both ways and then dug his hand into his crotch and pulled out a bunch of sweaty ass bills. They smelled worse than pigs rolling around in sewage. The stench went up my nose and made me gag before I then throw up out of the window.

Eve dry heaved and then opened the door to the van, throwing up all over the parking lot. "Get the fuck out of here." She pointed on her knees. "Go!

Now, before I pop yo' stanky ass." she promised before throwing up some more.

I rubbed my fingers under my arms to cake them with deodorant and shoved them up my nose. I couldn't breathe in peace. I needed to escape the scent of him.

The wind blew and this Hype continued to wave his money back and forth. "Aw, come on, shorty. Just give me my dope and I'll be on my way. I'm aching." He wrapped his arm around his stomach and leaned over with a pained look on his face.

I stepped out of the van and threw about nine foiled packs of heroin at him. "Take that shit and get the fuck out of here. If you come back smelling like that, I swear on my mother, I'ma smoke you, Boss. That's my word."

He kneeled and picked up each pack, and stood up with the money in his hand. "You want me to put this on the ground for you?" He smacked his crusty tips. There were large wet stains under each arm even though it was only thirty degrees outside.

Eve took her pistol and pointed it out the window. "Yo, take that stanking ass money, along with ya filthy ass, and get the fuck out of here, kid! Word up!"

He spun on his toes and took off running full speed out of the parking lot, looking over his shoulder every so often to see if we were chasing him or something.

When I got back into the van, Eve was spraying her perfume into the vents where the heat blew into the interiors. It smelled like Cherry Blossom. She took a stick of gum and popped it into her mouth, offering me a piece that I accepted. "Showbiz, I ain't trying to be out here selling bags forever. We need to step our game up and get on to some major paper. It seems like everybody else out here eating except us. We gotta change that shit." She took a blunt from the back of her ear and set fire to its tip.

I sat back in my seat and nodded. "I feel you, ma. But once I hit my uncle with this scratch, I got a feeling he gon' hit us off with a nice piece of dope for us to really get right. Then we can snatch up a few traps and get it in, you feel me?"

She shook her head. "N'all, fuck that. That's still thinking too small-minded. Ain't no major niggas out here pushing bags. That's for poo-butt muthafuckas that think they gon' get rich before Twelve snatch them up and toss they ass in prison but that rarely happens. It ain't a bunch a Jay-Z's in the city, Showbiz. Nah' mean?" She took a hit of the blunt, inhaled, and tried to pass it to me.

I pushed her hand away and groaned. "I'm straight on that shit. I still got a lil' Boy in my system. That weed ain't gon' do shit but give me a headache." I pulled my nose and closed my eyes for a brief second. "I feel what you saying, too. But you talking like you got some shit in mind. If you do, then let me know what's good. You know I'm down for that paper by any means."

She ran her tongue across her upper row of teeth. "If we fuck with my uncle out in Brooklyn, we can get paid twenty gees to murder niggas. That type of money adds up real fast. Shit, the way I feel, I ain't got love for nobody outside of you anyway, Showbiz. I'll murder niggas all day long and never get tired of it. There's something about seeing a nigga beg for his life before I put a bullet in his melon that make my pussy wet. I'm just being honest." She licked her juicy lips.

Hearing her talk like that made my dick harder than calculus. She had so much heart. That spit was a major turn on for me. I mean I knew she was just my homey, but damn, Eve was that real deal. "Yo, for twenty gees a head, I'll slump any nigga or bitch with no hesitation. My gun ain't ever prejudice. How can we get down with him?" I asked, feeling my stomach growl.

Eve smiled. "I'ma roll through there tonight and see what's good. He one of them crazy Jamaican niggas with a bunch of scores to settle. He run a gambling and loan sharking business on the side of his restaurant biz. In addition to all that, he takes contracts on mufuckas' heads. He was doing that shit back on the island and I guess, since he's been here, it's become even more profitable. Either way, I'ma get us down with him and we'll do our thing."

"Yo, that sounds like a plan. Eve, I ain't gon' even lie. When you was just talking about all of that murdering and shit, you had my dick hard as hell. I wanted you to jump up here and put in some work. You still ain't got me right from a few weeks back when you left me hanging after we slumped Max and nem."

She reached over and squeezed my dick. "Showbiz, this muhfucka always hard. Damn." She slid her hand into my pants and stroked it, playing with me.

My eyes rolled into the back of my hand. "Yo, stop doing that shit unless you about to let me fuck tonight. I'm not playing either." I humped into her hand and kept my eye out for any potential enemies but saw none. My Blood niggas were all over the place, stomping with puffy jackets on their backs and skull caps over their heads.

Eve leaned all the way over and sucked the head into her mouth and kissed it. "A'ight, let me stop then. Gon' head and put this muhfucka up." She smiled and sat back in her seat, sucking her fingers into her mouth.

Chapter 4

I didn't love nobody in this world the way I loved my mother. Her name was Amelia and she was my heart and soul. She was full-blooded Cuban but looked like a black woman from her hair to her skin color. She was 5'2" with brown eyes and weighed about 130 pounds soaking wet. It was two weeks after Eve and I had had the conversation about getting down with her uncle to murder niggas for that scratch, that my mother got the flu and needed me to care for her.

When I got there on one cold Wednesday night, I found her in her prayer room with candles burning all around her. She was kneeling in front of a picture of the Virgin Mary. She had her prayer beads in her right hand saying a prayer in Spanish.

I kneeled beside her and kissed her soft cheek after moving her long, thick, and curly hair out of her face. "I'm here, mama."

She continued to pray, nodding. She did the sign of the crucifix over my head and kissed my cheek. She didn't finish her prayers until ten minutes later. The whole time, I sat still and listened to her pray to God for the cleansing of my sins and those of the family. After she finished completely, I helped her up and she wrapped her arms around my neck.

"Hey, baby. What took you so long to get here?" she asked in Spanish. Well actually, my mother always spoke Spanish. She knew very little English and used it as less as she possibly could.

"I came as soon as I could get here, ma. You know I'd never put you on the back burner. You're my heart." I hugged her again and kissed all over her cheeks. This was my everything right here, the absolute Queen of my heart.

She placed a short blanket across her shoulders and stepped into the kitchen after coughing into her fists. "Your father and his men have fully taken over your grandfather's sugar cane fields. I heard that half of the five hundred acres have already been converted so they can produce cocaine and heroin. This will make the Vegas filthy rich, son. I need you to get closer to him because as the oldest, you are the first one that he should bless followed by Tristian and then Miguel." She opened the oven and pulled out a plate of fried chicken, white rice, pinto beans, and cornbread. She set it down on the stove and looked back at me. "Did you hear me?"

I was trying my best to mentally process everything. I couldn't fathom what 250 acres of dope looked like. I knew it meant we were about to be rolling, but it seemed so surreal to me. "Yes, I hear you, ma." I took the plate and walked to the table with it, pulled out my chair and took a seat. "Thank you for the food, ma. I thought you said that you had the flu?" I poured a homemade version of her hot sauce on my food and felt my stomach rumbling. It smelled so good.

My mother had pictures of Jesus and the Apostles all around her home. There were big paintings of the Virgin Mary nearly everywhere you looked, as well. She was very religious. Even though she was staying in the Bronx, she was all Cuban all the time and I loved her to death.

"The devil tried to make me sick with his flu, son, but after two days, I'm feeling better than ever. All that's left is a little cough. It's nothing that I can't deal with." She sat across from me. "Son, you have to conquer the Vegas and come into power before your father's many enemies strike and take him out. By the time that happens, you should be in full control of the Vega's throne." She smiled, reached across the table, and touched my hand.

I picked up a drumstick and nipped a big chunk of meat away with my teeth. The sauce mixed with the juiciness of the meat tasted so good, I had to close my eyes. "Ma, you know I'm on it. I just need to get my foot in the door so I can see what's going down. Once I do, you know my street smarts will kick in and I'll take over. I've always been that way."

"Sometimes it takes more than street smarts, son. Your father is a very emotional and cerebral man. If you can tap into his emotions, you can get him to see that you are the son that he needs to prep for his seat whenever he decides to step down. Then all he builds will be yours, baby. You were born to be a conqueror. You are my son and I believe in you with all that I am. You're twice as good as that bitch, Debra's son," she spat. Yeah, my mother was a religious woman, but that didn't mean that she didn't have an animal inside of her.

There was no other person on earth that could get under my mother's skin worse than Debra, my father's black baby mother. Debra had been the reason my father, Chico, had left my mother. She was a beautiful, ambitious, African American woman that, for the most part, had my father pussy-whipped. My mother hated her and him for allowing her to have such a hold on him.

I laughed. "Ain't nobody like me, ma. I'm my own man. You made sure to raise me as an individual and I appreciate you for that. Tristian ain't on my level in any way, shape, form or fashion. He ain't nothing but a soft college boy. He wouldn't know the first thing about taking Pop's seat whenever my dad decides to step down."

Tristian was my younger half-brother. I was older than him by three years. Debra was his mother and as much as I hated to admit it, my father favored him more than he did me and my full brother, Miguel. I thought it was because out of all of his sons, Tristian had been the only one to graduate from high school and enroll into college, knocking it out of the park. I didn't know for sure but at least, it's what I thought.

In all actuality, I didn't really care for Tristian or saw him as being a threat. And it didn't help that our mothers were beefing. I didn't give a fuck if my mother was in the right or the fact that every nigga outside of me was wrong. I was riding with her against anybody. That's just the way it was.

My mother came and placed her hand on my shoulder. "Baby, do whatever you need to do to get into your father's good graces. We'll need that seat. It's owed to us and it's the least he can do since he left us to fend for ourselves all of these years. I swear had it not been for the children that God gave me through him, I would regret the day I ever met that man."

I wiped my mouth on a napkin, stood up, and pulled her into my arms. "Don't have any regrets, mama. I got this. We can't give my father all of that power. We're smarter than he will ever be. You've told me that my entire life, remember?"

She smiled and looked up at me. "It's amazing all of the things you remember that I've said to you. You're such a good boy, Juanito. I'm glad that you have my middle name and none from him. He doesn't deserve such a son." She kissed both of my cheeks and rubbed my chest, getting lost deep within her thoughts. Then she snapped out of it and shook her head real hard. "Go ahead and finish your food, baby. I need you to help me with a few things around the house. I got some heavy boxes I need brought up from the basement that I need you to get for me. I also need you to run to the pharmacy to get my medication. You hear me?"

I picked up my drumstick and bit into it again. "I got you, ma."

* * *

That night, I pulled up on Tristian just as he was coming out of his brownstone in Brooklyn. He had one of his muscular arms around Kalani. I knew her to be his high school sweetheart. Tristian was about 6'1" and 190 pounds with light brown eyes like myself. He had a low cut with real deep, natural ocean waves. He was caramel with dimples.

And even though he was a college boy, when it came down to it, I'd seen him bust his gun time and time again. I still felt like he was soft because he had a problem with murdering anybody that didn't piss him off. He was one of those types that could only murder if they were angry enough to do so. I couldn't honor those type of hittas.

You were either a killer all the time or you was pussy in my book. But he was my little brother, so I had to tolerate him. I mean I did have a lil' love for him, but not the kind that most siblings had. If ever he got out of line, I wouldn't have a problem busting his brain.

I beeped my horn twice and rolled down my passenger's window. "Yo, Tristian. What it do, son?"

He laughed with his fists in front of his face, took his arm from around Kalani, and jogged down the stairs over to my whip. He sat his forearms on the windowsill. "What it do, big bruh? What brings you all the way out to Brooklyn? I ain't think you ever left Harlem, kid." I could smell his cologne drift into the car. It smelled like Cool Water.

I sat back in the driver's seat. "I come to fuck with you, but I can see you busy. I guess I can stroll back through at another time. No biggie."

The sun was just setting. It felt as if it were about forty degrees outside with barely any wind. I looked past Tristian's shoulder and saw Kalani wrap her arm around his waist before laying her head on his shoulder. Kalani was fine as a muthafucka and strapped. She was about 5'4" with caramel skin and brown eyes. She had long, wavy hair that fell past her shoulders. She weighed about 120 or 125 pounds, slightly pigeon-toed.

Looking at her, I'd been wanted to fuck that pussy since the first day my brother had introduced us. I could tell by the way she could never look me in the eyes that she felt a nigga, too. I mean I had never went at any bitch he fucked with out of respect of us being brothers, but I was willing to make an exception for her. Word up.

"Aw, it's good, Showbiz. I was gon' take my lady out to dinner and probably chill at the Pier after that for a lil' while. It's been a minute since we left the crib and did anything on the romantic side, so I'm just trying to step my game up a lil' bit. She deserve it." He kissed her cheek.

Kalani smiled and closed her eyes. She opened them and looked right down to me before diverting them away. "Baby, I mean if you wanna kick it with your brother for a lil' while, it's cool. Just don't be out all night. Maybe y'all can chill for an hour or so and I'll knock out this thesis that I gotta turn in by Monday."

Kalani was in college, as well. I forgot what she was going for exactly, but I knew it had something to do with business. I remember Tristian bragging on the fact that him and his woman were well on their way to getting their degrees. It made me feel sick on the stomach. I didn't have the patience for all of that kind of shit. I wanted my money and my success as soon as possible. I had problems with authority and I wasn't the best test taker when I was in school. I always felt dumb and a little slower than everybody else when they understood something in class I couldn't quite get.

Tristian hugged her. "Yeah, let me fuck with him for an hour, baby. Then we'll go out on the town. I promise it won't take no longer than that, okay?"

She nodded. "A'ight, but you make sure you keep your word. I'm timing yo' ass." She walked away with her tight Fendi jeans all in her ass. Her cheeks jiggled with each step she took. Before she placed her foot on the first step, she turned around and caught me looking. She smiled and made her way up the stairs.

I was hard as a rock looking at all of that ass. I bit my lower lip and shook my head. "Kid, I know you killing that ass, right?"

Tristian opened my passenger's door and slid into the Monte Carlo SS before closing it back. He looked out of the window at her until she disappeared into the house. "Yo, that's my baby right there. I been doing my thing for more than four years now, so I'm well acquainted with her jewels, kid. That's my pussy, word up." He pulled his seatbelt around him. "So, what brings you out here to Brooklyn, Dunn?"

I laughed him off. I didn't give a fuck what he'd just said, I ain't think he was hitting shorty the way he needed to. She was so thick, that a muhfucka would have to put in some serious work. I was sure of that. I had to shrug it off just to regain my focus.

"Look, I got word that Pops just gained full possession of the Vega's fields and he turning half of it into heroin and cocaine plants. If that's the case, we about to be rich, nigga. You know that, right?" I needed to feel him out to see where his head was at. Tristian was always talking about being something bigger and better than a drug lord. If that was the case, then this move by our father shouldn't have excited him at all.

He shrugged. "It was bound to happen. He was telling me about him taking over the fields last year, so if you ask me, it's long overdue. As far as us becoming rich because of this, who knows. I ain't gon' get excited about it until it actually happens. But whether it does or not, I'ma figure shit out for myself. I don't need Pops for more than what he's already provided for me. This education is everything."

I pulled away from the curb and exhaled loudly. "A'ight, nigga. I don't want to spend a whole night talking about this shit again. I get it, you're in school. Now, can we please move on?"

Tristian mugged me and looked out of his passenger's window. "Anyway, you must got something on your mind, so let me hear it."

I shook my head. "Just wanted to give you a heads up, that's all. If Pops already got some of that shit up and running, I got plans to flood New York, kid. I'm talking all five boroughs. Get some of that real money that changes a nigga's life. I'm tired of rocking this Monte Carlo. I want something foreign that'll hurt niggas' feelings and make bitches wet just off the paint job. I want to go hard for about six months, then open up a few clubs throughout the Big Apple. That's where the money is. Once I get my chips right, I'ma buy my mother a whole house and fully furnish it. Yeah, that's what's good."

I smiled just imagining what that would feel like. If I could put my mother in her own home, I'd feel like I'd accomplished something worthwhile. She deserved the absolute best of the best if you asked me.

Tristian was quiet. He looked out of his window as if on high alert. "I don't doubt none of that shit you talking about, Showbiz. I know you're a trapper, but you gotta get shit in order so when that hustling shit goes south, you'll be able to fall back on your legit money. That's what real hustlers do. They use that drug money as a stepping stone to something greater that will last for a long, long time. That's what we gotta do."

I agreed, but I didn't say it out loud. I didn't like encouraging Tristian to kick that knowledge shit because whenever I did, he had a habit of kicking it all the time and that became annoying as fuck. "Well, anyway, you know how Pops is. By him busting this new move, he gon' want to have a sit down with us just to bring us up to speed. Just be prepared. If you ain't trying to be down, then I would suggest you tell him that right away. He don't need to put large quantities of that shit in your hand if you ain't ready to twerk that shit. Nah'mean?"

To be honest, I just wanted Tristian out of the mix. Whatever my father was about to lay on us, I felt like I could handle Tristian's share and my own if it came down to it. I had Eve as my right hand and together, we could make it happen. I thought, as I pulled back in front of Tristian's stoop.

He laughed, "Nall, I ain't graduated yet, nigga. If Pops gon' drop something heavy in my lap, I'ma figure out how to work that shit. I like money just like the next man. I just ain't about to get addicted to the life because for me, it's temporary."

I nodded my head. "That's what's up. Well, I guess I'll see you in a few days. I'ma reach out to our old man and see what's good. I tried this morning but he ain't returned my calls or texts yet." I was still irritated by that fact. Usually when I text my Pops or called him, he made it his business to get back at me within the next hour after I did.

Tristian frowned. "That's odd. I was just talking to him before me and Kalani left the house. He's over in DC taking care of some business with the Block Boy Cartel. He's supposed to work his way back out here tonight or tomorrow morning at the latest. Wait a second." He pulled out his phone and dialed our father's number, then switched it to speaker phone.

The phone rang for three times, then I heard my father's deep voice. "What's up, mijo?"

Mijo was what my father referred to me and my brothers as. In Spanish, it meant my son.

Tristian spoke to him in Spanish. "Pop, I got Juanito right here. He says that he's been trying to get a hold of you."

"Hey, Juanito. I'm sorry, mijo. I've been busy trying to get things in order where I am. Is there a reason you're trying to track me down?" he asked, before coughing for a few seconds.

I curled my lip and felt my temper run hot. The fact that he'd answered his phone for Tristian in a matter of three rings, while he'd usually made me wait for an hour or more, really attested to the fact that he favored my younger brother more than he did me. It was hurtful and insulting. It was one of the reasons I resented him the way I did.

"You know what, Pop, I'm good. You just finish handling whatever you're handling. When the time is right, I figure you'll have a sit down with your sons. Until then, be safe out there." I waved Tristian's phone away from me. I was disgusted.

"Okay, mijo. I just want you to know that it is nothing personal. I love the both of you and I'll be seeing you very soon." He disconnected his call.

"Bruh, you a'ight?" Tristian asked, looking me over closely.

I nodded and pulled on my nose. I needed a fix. My stomach felt like it was being punched over and over again. I was seconds away from throwing up.

"I'm good, bruh. I'm gon' go ahead and make my way back over to Harlem before it gets too late. You know these Brooklyn niggas don't like the god. I been heating they ass up ever since I learned how to buck a pistol." I laughed and threw my car in park. "I'ma fuck with you at another time, bruh. Love, fool." I leaned over and gave him a quick hug.

Kalani stepped out of their brownstone and looked down at my whip, waiting for Tristian to step out of it. Her thick thighs were prominent in those jeans. That girl was something else.

"A'ight, Dunn. Well, I'll catch you in a minute. Hold ya head out here and stay alert. That devil something serious, kid."

"Yo, I'll empty my whole clip at Satan's ass, word up. I ain't letting him take the god without a fight. I'll catch you later, though." I waited until he stepped out of the car and closed the door before I beeped my horn twice and skirted away from the curb.

Chapter 5

I leaned down and tooted the lines of China White, picked my head up and held my nose. The drug rushed through me like a hurricane, numbing every portion of my body. I felt like I could hear chapel bells in my ears. My heart was pounding so fast, I could barely breathe. But at the same time, a calming, euphoric feeling swept over me. I felt giddy and ready to buss a move.

Eve sat on the side of me. She slammed a clip into her .45 and cocked it back. She closed one eye and aimed it at the wall as if ready to hit a target. Her teeth bit into her bottom lip and she looked like a sexy ass gangsta bitch, Harlem fed and Harlem bred. "Showbiz, he gon' give us twenty thousand a piece to slump these niggas. I'm finna put that lil' bread towards my whip. Hector got a pink and black Audi S6 that I just gotta have. He want fifteen for it.

I'ma drop that paper like a bad habit so I can be riding clean when the spring hits in a few weeks. I'm tired of jumping out that El, or having you to come and get me all of the time." She set the gun on the table and grabbed her plate of China White, took a red straw and tooted about a half gram of it. Pinching her nose, she tilted her head back with her eyes closed.

I was so high, I felt like the room was spinning. My body was vibrating. I could feel my veins throbbing in my arms. "Yo, as long as your uncle gon' drop that bread, I don't care who I gotta smoke or how many. At twenty gees a pop, I'll stank a whole crowd of muhfuckas and cash the check later. Word is bond." I sniffed and wiped my nose with the cloth sitting next to my plate of dope.

We were chilling in Eve's basement with a red bulb in. I grabbed one of the .45s and slammed clip inside of it. "Why he saying we gotta use these for Nickeli? Why we can't use our own heat?" I asked, looking my pistol over. I really didn't have a problem knocking a nigga shit loose with a .45, but I found it odd that he wanted us to use those guns in particular.

Eve undid two of the buttons on her blouse, exposing a hint of her cleavage. She dabbed a few beads of sweat that decorated them. My dick started to get hard as hell. She shrugged. "I don't know, Showbiz. He just do shit his own way. We can't get to asking a bunch of questions. We gotta keep shit simple and let this add up, nah'mean, kid?" She licked her juicy lips and lowered her eyes, looking across the table at me.

I knew that every time she got that dope in her system, her pussy got red hot. I was imagining my dick going in and out of her hole and my shit started to hop up and down. "Yo, Eve. Let me see you model that skirt real quick. I wanna peep them thick ass thighs for a minute while I pull on this dick. My word, you got me over here feenin' or your lil' sexy ass."

She licked her lips and squeezed her breasts together. "What, you checking me out from across the table and shit?" She undid two more buttons. Her brown, creamy titties exposed themselves. She leaned forward and pushed her plate of raw to the side.

"Check this out, Showbiz. If I let you fuck this pussy real quick, you gon' have to murder this shit. I'd love to put two in a nigga's face while my tunnel is aching. I need some good dick right now and I know you will dope dick the shit out of me if I let you. Won't you?" She undid the rest of the buttons and pulled her blouse out of her skirt. Now her breasts were free. They looked like two ripe melons with hard nipples that stood out an inch a piece.

I made my way around to her side so fast that I don't even remember getting up. I placed my hands under her arms and sat her on the table. "Yo, give me some of this shit, ma." I yanked her skirt all the way up to her hips, and forced her thick thighs apart before grabbing the chair that she was sitting in, taking a seat.

I scooted closer and sniffed her box. It smelled like Burberry perfume with nice hint of pussy. I pushed my nose inside of her dark brown lips and inhaled as hard as I could. There was nothing like the natural scent of a woman. That shit drove me crazy. I would sniff some clean pussy all day long and never get tired of it. I peeled her lips apart. Her pinkness glistened in the red light of the basement. I kissed her right in the center of them and slurped up her juices. I was sucking out of her fountain as if I was starving for her essence.

She cocked her legs open further apart across the table. "Lick my ass too, Showbiz. Get all that shit wet. I'm finna let you hit every hole I got on my body. You know how we get down. It's gang-gang, nigga. Word up." She sucked her bottom lips into her mouth and pulled on her long nipples. "Uh! That shit feel so good."

I peeled her ass cheeks apart and licked around her anus. She had just a hint of hair there. I could feel it on my tongue. I slid my tongue inside and fucked it in and out of her body. Then I licked all the way upward and trapped her clit with my lips, sucking on it so good, she began to buck into my mouth. "You like that shit, Blood. Let me know it," I said, licking up and down her crease, making loud, nasty noises.

She spread her lips further apart and closed her eyes. "This dope got me horny, Showbiz. I need you to fuck me right now. I don't need you to eat me. Uh! But fuck, it feel so good!" She rotated her hips in a circular motion with her tongue resting on the left side of her mouth.

I nipped at the clit, sucked it, and then slid my tongue as deep into her pussy as it could go before repeating the same process. I needed to taste her cum on my tongue before I beat that pussy into submission. For some reason, whenever I could taste a bitch's pussy on my tongue while I fucked her, it caused that animal to come out of me.

It was like rubbing cocaine over your gums after you'd finished tooting a pile of the shit. I put my middle finger up her ass and ran it in and out of her tight back door and kept sucking at her clitoris while she rode my face like I owed her some money.

"Eat that pussy, Showbiz. Eat that pussy! Aww, fuck. You finna make me cum. You finna make me cum!" She wrapped her thick thighs around my face and rode me until she came all over my mouth, pulling her own nipples. Her stream ran all down my neck and slid into my wife beater.

I licked and bit all over her thick thighs leaving teeth marks across them. She was so fucking strapped. That Puerto Rican and Jamaican made a perfect blend. Like it even affected how good she tasted but then again, I might have been exaggerating even though I didn't think so. After she came, she hopped off of the table with her skirt still around her waist. She walked me backward to the couch where I sat and watched her stand in front of me. Her pussy peaked from between her thighs. It looked like a mini booty or something.

She ran her finger between her lips. "I'm wanna ride that dick, Showbiz, but first let me suck you for a minute. Fair exchange ain't robbery." She kneeled and took a hold of my dick. She pumped it and ran the big head across her cheek. She licked around it and sucked me into her mouth. From there, her face became a blur as she tightened her lips and speared her mouth on me again and again, making slurping sounds that were full of spit and suction.

My toes curled right up. I grabbed a handful of her curly hair and allowed my eyes to roll into the back of my head. That shit felt so good. "Damn, ma. Damn, you doing ya thing. Gang-gang."

She suckled me faster and harder. She tightened her fist and opened her eyes to look me deep into my own. That shit turned me on even more. There was nothing like getting some boss ass head from a dime piece. Eve was super bad. On top of that, she was a straight killer just like me. All of those factors made head feel that much better. I had to push her face away from me or I was going to cum down her throat.

Her mouth exited my penis with a loud sucking sound. She looked up at me confused. "Why you stop me? I was just starting to taste your precum. That shit getting me geeked." She licked my head and kissed it.

I grabbed her hair and pulled her up and on top of me. She straddled my lap and humped into my dick. The stalk of my piece separated her lips but didn't enter her wet cat that was leaking like a busted pipe. I gripped her big ass and pulled the cheeks apart. "Put my dick in you, Eve. Come on, let's fuck like savages. Gang-gang style." She was more Blood crazy than I was and that was saying a lot. I bit into her neck. "Do it, bitch. Hurry up."

She leaned forward and grabbed my throbbing dick, wiggling around on the head before allowing it to sink into her pussy. I struggled to break into her pussy's hallway, but after some maneuvering, I was finally able to sink deep into her body. It felt like I was fucking a slab of hot ass ground beef or something. I mean she was real meaty in there and tight. Her walls sucked at me.

I grabbed that ass and pulled her forward. "Uh! Uh! Fuck! Yes! Shit! Damn! This pussy so good," I groaned as she worked her hips back and forth.

"Yes, Juanito. Yes! Uh fuck, yes!" She bounced on my dick with her eyes closed. She sucked all over my lips and licked them before biting into my neck with her teeth. "Aww, Juanito! Fuck me, daddy! Yes!" She picked up speed and rode me faster and faster. She licked all over my neck and dug her nails into my shoulder blades.

I was sucking on her hard nipples until they would fall out of my mouth from her movement. My hand rubbed all over her ass and I was trying to slip my middle finger into her back door. I was fucking that ass before we were done and I wasn't taking no for an answer.

"Ride. This. Dick. Eve. Faster, ma. Aww, fuck! Faster, shorty." I could feel my dick beating at her walls. It felt like she was trying to grip it with her kitty muscles. The couch kept scooting further and further backward.

"I got you. I got you. I got you, daddy. Aww, shit. I got you," she moaned, bouncing higher and higher. She licked all over my lips and moaned with her cheek against mine.

I stood up and wrapped my arms around her waist, bouncing her at full speed. I was trying to stuff her with everything that I had.

"Aw! Aw! Aw! Aw! Aw! Oh, shit! Kill this shit! Kill it! Aww, yes!" she moaned, putting her tongue in my ear canal, licking all around it.

I crashed into the wall with her, still bouncing her thick ass. I could feel the head of my dick tingling like crazy. I didn't know how much more of that pussy I could take without shooting up her womb. "Eve, Eve, Eve. I'm 'bout, to, cum, in, this, pussy," I gasped, killing her against the wall. I was lifting her by her ass cheeks and getting the deepest part of her womb like that.

"Do it, Showbiz! Do it! Please, cum in me! Daddy! Aww, fuck!" She dug her nails into my shoulders again and screamed. Her inner walls began to vibrate and spit her cum all over my head.

I bounced her faster and faster with my knees bent, then I was cumming deep in her pussy while I smashed her body against the wall, sucking all over her pretty titties.

She quivered and after two minutes, got down on wobbly legs. "Fuck, that was good, Showbiz. Now I'm ready to kill up some shit." She ran her finger up and down her slit and looked up at me with sweat across her forehead.

My dick was jumping like crazy. I had my eyes on her gap. Her meaty pussy looked real good to me. She turned around and picked her blouse up off the floor. Her ass cheeks jiggled, and that was almost too much. I grabbed her by the hair and pushed her over the arm of the couch.

"What the fuck are you doing, Juanito? Get off of me," she growled, slapping at my hand. "You're hurting me."

I kicked her legs apart and rubbed my dick head up and down her slit to lubricate it. I sucked my middle finger into my mouth and fingered her ass. "I gotta get me some of this. Ain't no way I'm finna be able to go out and slump some shit with you if I can't get this fat booty off of my mind. You already know how I am." I pulled her cheeks apart and placed my head on her hole, slowly forcing it into her backdoor.

She tightly closed her eyes and reached under her body, taking ahold of her pearl tongue, pinching it and opening her sex lips. "You always trying to take some shit, Juanito. Damn, you make me sick. Aww, fuck yes," she moaned, humping back on me.

I pumped forward and broke into the hallway of her backdoor. It was so tight, I felt suffocated. "Uh! Uh! Uh! Uh! Yeah! Yeah! Gimme this ass. Gimme this shit! Yeah. Damn, shorty!" I started to pipe her ass down. The harder I fucked it, the more she played with her clitoris.

Her juices ran down both of her thighs. She held her sex lips apart, exposing her pink pussy. "Yes, Juanito. Kill me! Kill! Me! Uh fuck! You so deep! You so deep! Shit!" she hollered, looking back at me with sweat dripping off of her little cute nose.

We made eye contact and that caused me to really murder that ass like a savage. I pulled on her hair and spanked her cheeks, rocking her until I came deep within her bowels. We fell to the floor with her rubbing her box like crazy, humping into the air. I sucked on her nipples until she came again, whimpering in Spanish.

T.J. Edwards

Chapter 6

I blew my nose on the Kleenex and tossed it into the trashcan beside the leather couch we were sitting on. The lights were dimmed. In front of us was a round table made of oak wood. On top of it was a bottle of Ciroc and a bottle of Moet sitting in a bucket of ice. I had a Cuban cigar in my right hand and my left arm was draped around Eve. She had her head on my shoulder playing the role of Wifey.

We were at the Forty-Forty club for a listening party. There was so much weed smoke in the air, it looked like we were inside of a cloud. The club had about fifteen more people inside of it and all were in their own sections enjoying their privacy. Eve's uncle had set it up for us to be able to attend some new rapper's listening party.

He called himself Yotti and he was supposed to be our mark for the night along with his manager. I didn't know why they were the targets, but what I did know was that I was ready to blast some shit. I could barely contain myself.

Eve nuzzled into my neck as Yotti took the stage. "Yo, that's who we capping right there. His manager is that lil' Jewish muthafucka standing by the stage near the exit. I'll have some of him. I like killing them white boys. Their deaths don't affect me the way hood niggas do." She kissed my neck.

My trigger finger was itching. I would smoke either one. I didn't care, just as long as I got to spill one of them. "Yo, that's cool. Where you wanna catch they ass at?" I asked as Yotti got to nodding his head on stage. They'd dropped an instrumental and I guessed he took that as his cue to begin spitting.

She grabbed the bottle of Moet and poured some into her champagne glass, filling it up to the brim. She picked it up and drank half of it. "Veto say he want us to empty all twenty shots in these fools, so we gotta catch them somewhere where we'll be able to do that. Not in the club, though. Maybe out back by their whip or something. I just know we have to make every shot count."

I sipped out of the bottle of Ciroc and burped. "I guess we'll figure it out. One thing's for sure, it's gon' be hell sitting back listening to this whack ass nigga spit a whole album. My word, son sound like he just picked up the mic." I shook my head in disgust and wrapped my arm back around her shoulder. I could still smell the scent of her pussy on my upper lip. Even though I'd showered, I'd purposely left that there. I sniffed and smiled.

There were a bunch of females holding up their phones and filming the stage while he rapped and did his thing. I didn't see what all of the hype was about, but I leaned back and scanned the club. There were two big dudes with black jackets on that said "Security" on the back of them. They looked over the club and made sure that everything was cool and in order. They looked like ex-football players or something. Big black niggas with folds on the backs of their baldheads.

A short distance away from them was two more men huddled together talking. They had earpieces in their ears and laptops in their hands. They looked like record producers. Behind them were four fine model-looking sistas that were sipping champagne and smoking fat blunts of Kush. They nodded their heads at the lyrics that Yotti was spitting. They wore lip gloss so thick, it sparkled in the dim lights. I looked around the rest of the club and saw costly couples hugged up, doing their own choice of drugs. It was a typical listening party out in New York City where most niggas got their start.

Eve sat back and crossed her thick thighs. The Prada skirt rose on her legs and exposed their silky smoothness. "Damn, it's some fine hoes up in here. I should take one of these niggas' bitches. I know it wouldn't be a task," she joked, looking around. She grabbed the bottle of Moet and sipped out of it, licking around the rim. "You think I would?"

I shrugged my shoulders. "I don't know. These lil' hoes look stuck up and all about they paper. You fine and all but they can tell from a mile away that you ain't got enough to pay they condo's rent every month, along with their car notes and whatever other expenses they may have. These bitches look like they all about their riches. Word up." I kissed her neck. "But besides the money aspect of things, you definitely wouldn't have a problem taking their bitches. I'll stand on that."

She shook her head. "I sho' ain't paying no bitch's rent or car note. They got me fucked up to the max. The most I'll do for a hoe is let her eat this pussy and pay her Uber fare. After that, it's a wrap like Reynold's. Nah' mean?" She laughed.

Yotti had stopped spitting and now his track was playing over the speakers of the club. It had grown cloudier inside of it. I could smell the different

Ganjas in the air. I felt like I needed to treat my nose, and by the way Eve was pulling on hers, I could tell that she was ready for a fix, too. "Yo, let's fuck with a couple grams while we listen to this fuck nigga spit this bullshit. Hopefully, it'll take the edge off."

She wiped her nose and sucked on her bottom lip. She had a habit of doing that. I found it sexy no matter how many times she did it in a day. "A'ight, that sounds cool. Shit, everybody else in here doing their thing anyway, ain't they?" she asked, looking around.

I slipped the China White out of my fatigue jacket designed by Marc Jacobs. The powder was in a thin, yellow envelope. I poured the contents onto a platter that was on our table and made four lines. I handed it to Eve first. "Here you go, ma."

She took a straw out of here purse and tooted one and then another, before holding her nose and sitting back on the couch. I grabbed the straw from her and did my thing. The dope rushed all over me right away, and the club became a movie to me. Even though it was my reality, none of it seemed real. I had a vision of standing up and bucking everybody in that bitch, except for Eve, of course. My mouth got dry and I felt instantly happy and horny.

I placed my hand on to Eve's thick thigh and squeezed it. The hem of her skirt had risen so far that I could see she wasn't wearing any panties. "Every time I fuck with this shit, Eve, it make me wanna eat yo' ass up." I bit her neck.

She pushed me away. "Nigga, that shit can wait 'til later. We gotta be on point. It's forty gees on the line. We gotta let these pistols talk, not your penis. I got bills to pay. Word is bond," she said, pulling the hem of her skirt down and wiping her mouth. She stood up and threw her long hair over her shoulders. "This nigga finna come off of this stage. I'm about to go and holler at him. Can't no man resist this Puerto Rican Jamaican. You can watch my ass as I walk away, though. I might let you hit it again, long as you handle yo' business tonight." She smiled and walked toward the stairs of the stage. Her skirt continued to rise as it cuffed her ass so perfectly. I could make out her bottom cheeks before she pulled it back down and looked over her shoulder at me.

She caught Yotti just as he was coming off of the stage. At first, his manager stepped in her path, but Yotti waved him off and brushed the small Jewish man aside. Yotti slid his arm around her neck and got to saying something in her ear. She laughed and patted him on the chest in a flirtatious manner.

I sat back on the couch and spread my arms out. The dope had me feeling real good. I licked my lips and scanned the club again. They had on a more up-tempo record that had the females up and popping their asses. I nodded my head at the track before scoping Eve and Yotti. Eve shook her head and pointed in my direction before waving me over. I pointed at myself as if asking if she was talking about me. She nodded, and waved me over once again. So, I stood up and instantly I felt like I got up too fast. The high came over me once again. I could hear the chapel bells in my ears. The back of my neck began to perspire. My stomach turned and then, all at once, that happy feeling came over me followed by one of exhaustion. I slowly made my way over to them.

Eve stepped up to me and hugged me, then slid her arm back around Yotti's lower back. "Kid, this is Yotti. Yotti, this is my big brother, Kid. He's from Virginia. He got skills, too, but he ain't trying to pursue no music career or nothing like that. He's a businessman. Soon, you might be the closing act in one of his clubs." Eve looked up and smiled at me.

Yotti extended his hand. He was about 5'6" with long dread locks and tattoos all over his face. He smelled a lil' rank and his clothes were so tight, I was wondering how this nigga was able to breathe. He was also real skinny like he never ate or something. "What's good, Kid?"

I shook my head. "Shit, just enjoying your tracks. You got talent, lil' bruh. I'd love to do business with you somewhere down the line." I shook his hand and then that of his manager.

The Jewish man was about 5'3", heavy-set with wavy hair, balding in the middle. He had an earpiece in his left ear and an iPhone in his right hand. "Nice to meet you, Kid."

"Likewise." I finished shaking his hand and looked down to Eve. "What's good, ma? Why y'all posted right here?"

Yotti snickered. "Yo, shorty say you got that China White. I'm trying to hit my nose a lil' bit so I can make it through the night. My manager will pay you whatever you taking for an ounce of that shit, long as it's good."

I made eye contact with Eve and she lowered hers and smiled. I nodded. "Yeah, a'ight. That sound good, but I ain't bring enough to sell. I can party with you though. I mean since you and my sister getting a lil' cozy and shit."

"A'ight, well I got the VIP room upstairs. We can go up there and do whatever. But after we do, I wanna spend some alone time with this lil' thick one right here." He grabbed her ass and rubbed all over it. "What you think about that, baby girl?"

I actually saw her cringe. I knew that Eve hated whenever a man that didn't know her called her baby girl or touched her in any way without her permission. The whole time her brother Charlie had been molesting her, he'd always call her baby girl throughout the process. So, I knew that name brought back a lot of painful memories for her. Ever since we'd been cool, I'd never called her that.

She sucked her teeth and looked up to Yotti. "You know what, Kid? I know I said that I'd make sure that his manager was straight, but I change my mind. I wanna take care of Yotti in my own special way." She smiled and eyed him. "Say, Yotti. Don't you got a limo or something? I mean how are you living, baby?" She placed her hand on his chest and stroked it. His music continued to blare out of the speakers.

He nodded his head. "Hell yeah, I got the stretch out back. What? Y'all wanna party in there, and then you and I can get to know each other on our own upstairs?" He ran his tongue across his lips looking her up and down.

"That sound like a plan to me."

Even though I knew we were on a mission, every part of me wanted to knock this nigga's head off. I didn't like the way he was treating Eve. I didn't like this nigga touching her or being in her presence for the length of time that he had been. I was extremely overprotective of her, even though I knew she could hold her own. I still felt like she was my Lil' One.

Eve kissed him on the cheek. "Yeah, let's do it that way. My brother gotta go handle some shit in a lil' while anyway. Would you have a problem dropping me off after we're done?" she asked, batting her eyelashes at him.

"Where are you from? I can have my driver take you anywhere you need to go."

"I'm from the Bronx. About twenty blocks away from here."

He nodded and slid his arm around her shoulder, kissing her neck. "The world is yours, ma. How can I turn down something so fucking bad? I can't." He laughed again and took her hand. "Come on."

Minutes later, we all got into the back of his stretch Navigator. Eve sat beside him, and his manager sat beside me. There was a small table in the middle of us. I took the heroin out of my pocket and dumped out about a half ounce on to the table.

I separated it into twelve thick lines and handed Yotti a rolled up hundred-dollar bill. "Huh, you go ahead and get your roll on first. I guarantee you love this shit. It's about ninety percent."

Yotti took the bill and put it into his nostril. He turned his head to the side and tooted a line into his right nostril. He sat up and rubbed his finger around the inside of it, shaking his head. "Damn, that shit hit hard right there." He leaned down and treated his other nostril before passing the bill to Eve.

She took it and handed it to his manager. "N'all, we always let our company go first. It's how we get down on the south side of the Bronx."

His manager took the bill and tooted two quick lines. Held his nose and sat back on the seat with his eyes closed. "Fuck, that's some good shit right there." He handed the bill back to Yotti.

"Say, Yotti. Where is your driver? I thought you said you had a driver that would take her anywhere she needed to go."

The manager laughed and waved me off. "You've already met the driver. I am him, and he is me." He opened his eyes and then closed them back, scratching at his neck.

Yotti tooted another line and fell back on the couch. He kissed Eve on the neck again and licked it. "When we get back upstairs, I'ma show you what the Yotti effect is all about." He placed his hand on her thigh and tried to slide it upward. Eve took a hold of his wrist to stop him. I could tell that she was struggling. She made a lot of noises as she fought against his strength.

His manager opened his eyes and began to laugh. "Aw, shit. Here we go. Every time you get that dope in your system, Yotti, you gotta take some pussy."

I watched Eve get her hand into her Gucci bag. She rummaged around inside of it for a brief second as Yotti's hand went all the way up her skirt. She yelped and came out of her purse with the .45 and slammed it under his chin. Before the shots rang out, I smiled and leaned down to toot a line.

Boom! Boom! Boom!

Brains bust out of Yotti's head and stuck to the ceiling of the limo before dropping to the carpet beneath it. I could smell the gun smoke from her gun as I finished my line.

"You punk ass nigga! You thought it was sweet!" Eve yelled and threw his dead body to the floor. She put the barrel into his eye socket and pulled the trigger again two times.

Boom! Boom!

The fire from her gun illuminated the dimly lit limo's interior.

His manager must've thought he was tripping. He opened and then closed his eyes tightly. He shook his head from side to side. "No, no, no. This can't be happening. I'm fucking tripping. I'm tripping. What did you put in this heroin, man?" he asked.

I elbowed him in the jaw, turned with my gun already out and placed my gun to his temple, pulling the trigger three times.

Boom! Boom! Boom!

Knocking three big holes into the side of his head, his brain matter sprayed the windows of the car and leaked down the sides. He fell onto his face with his eyes wide open. I placed the gun to the back of his head and emptied the clip, fingerfucking the trigger while I bit into my bottom lip. Eve did the same to Yotti before we stepped out into the dark parking lot and fled the scene.

Chapter 7

Eve and I went on a major killing spree for the next eleven months, grossing no less than $40,000 a move that we always split down the middle. I started to pack the safes that I had at my other cribs. I was trying to get my weight all the way up so I could put some of my Blood niggas on out in Spanish Harlem. Since I felt like my old man was on some fuck shit, I completely ignored his calls and decided I'd do my own thing. I didn't need him to get to where I wanted to be in the game. In fact, with the way I was feeling, had there ever came a time where I would've caught him slipping and able to hit his ass for a ton of that Vega heroin, I would've done it with no remorse.

I didn't give a fuck about him, my brothers, or no other man that walked this green earth. As far as I was concerned, the only people that mattered were my mother, Eve, Punkin, and my son, Maine. He was born on June 21st of that year. He came into the world weighing in at 6 pounds and 11 ounces. He had my eyes and hair, but his mother's face and likeness. Around the time he was born, I still didn't even know if I was ready for a kid. I was in the streets real heavy, and on top of that, Punkin and me wasn't on the best of terms.

The pregnancy had been extremely hard on her. She was made to stay in the hospital for three months after the birth of our son, and in the first week of the fourth, she passed away. What's crazy is that it didn't affect me in any emotional way. I think during the pregnancy we argued so much, I'd honestly lost any form of an emotional attachment to her. I know that may sound bogus as hell, but it's the truth.

Our relationship, after I found out she was pregnant, consisted of nothing but constant arguments and frustration. I didn't even show up to the funeral. In my mind, a funeral was for grieving. I didn't feel as if I had anything to grieve. When her sister, Ebony, stepped in and said she wanted to take custody of Maine, I didn't even fight her on it. My mind wasn't right, so I let her take him and gave her $20,000. I then made her a promise that whenever I was ready to get my son back that she would hand him over to me without a fight. She agreed and we put it in writing.

That same week, I held a meeting with four of my young Bloods. My uncle Javier had shipped me twenty kilos of pure Vega heroin for my birthday. He told me they were from my father and that I should get in contact with him. It was important. I blew it off and wound up breaking down the kilos with Eve and four of my young Bloods.

The one I fucked with the most was named Wetto. He was a full-blooded Cuban like me and the leader of the young Dyckman Bloods. He was 5'8", about 250 pounds solid. He had tattoos all over his face and kept a red rag around his neck. I'd been in action with him twice before and could confirm that he was a straight killer.

I'd watched him blow a man's head right off of his neck with a shotgun just because he was wearing the color blue. Wetto was my type of nigga. I had plans of using him to funnel my dope into the young

Bloods and therefore, into the Dyckman houses out in Harlem.

We sat at my kitchen table with Ziploc bags full of packaged heroin all across the table. He had a big blunt in his mouth. His eyes were squinted because of the smoke coming from the Cuban.

"I want to see you niggas eating with me, son. Word is bond. I'm putting a lot of faith into you, Wetto. But I know you got me. That Cuban shit runs deep in your veins just like it does mine." I laced another Ziploc bag and stacked it on the table.

Wetto took the blunt out of his mouth and sat it in the ashtray. "We're about to turn these projects out, kid. That's my word. I got fifty of my young niggas that's gon' twerk Harlem with me. Before you know it, it won't be shit moving through this bitch without your stamp of approval. I got this, Blood. Just trust me and let me handle shit like I know I can," Wetto said, picking the blunt back up and taking four deep pulls from it, inhaling and cheesing at the same time.

I grunted and looked into his eyes with my head slightly tilted. "Trust is earned and never given up front, son. Yo, I'm letting you know right now, kid. I ain't gone hesitate to buss yo' head if my dough ever begin to look funny. I'm putting shit in your hands, which means that you're responsible. Not none of these other niggas." I slammed my hand on the table, and lowered my eyes, mugging him. "You get that?"

I wanted to make sure that we had an understanding. I already knew where Wetto's mother laid her head, along with his daughter and baby mother, as well. If it ever came down to it, and he fell out of line, I would smoke all three of them, and then track his ass down, putting a few hot ones in him, as well. I was Gang-Gang, but nothing came before my money. I would kill Wetto with no hesitation and wouldn't lose a wink of sleep.

Wetto sat the blunt back in the ashtray and flared his nostrils. He looked into my eyes and blew the smoke through his nose. Sweat appeared on his bald-head where a bunch of tattoos were. "Yo, I don't fuck with no nigga's scratch. Especially not one of my own. Not only are you one of my Blood niggas, but you're from the motherland. Your blood is pure. You bleed deep within my veins, Son. I'd fuck over a hun-nit niggas before I'd ever consider fucking over you. The Vega's name ring bells back home, kid. I got a lot of respect for you and your family. Believe the god when I tell you that."

Eve took out her .9 millimeter and politely set it on the table. She turned the barrel toward Wetto and sucked her teeth. I noted that the three other Blood niggas that came with Wetto tensed up, but they did-n't make a move.

"Yo, Wetto. That's my mans right there. I don't like the way you all up in his face. It's in your best interest to fall back just a little bit or I can't be held responsible for what happens to you." She ran her tongue across her teeth and scrunched her face.

Wetto laughed and sat back in his seat. "Yo, word through the projects is that you two muthafuckas are looney. I couldn't really see that shit from a distance but now that I'm actually in front of the both of you, I can confirm that to be the truth. I love this shit, though. I would prefer to work under no other killers than you two. That's my word."

I took five of the packaged kilos and slammed them in front of him as Eve put her gun back on her hip. "A'ight then, I want fifty a piece. You knock these bitches out of the park, and I'll hit you with five more. You're the only one that got my number, Wetto. Don't give it to nobody else. Throughout this whole process, I'm gone only fuck with you and vice versa. I implore you to get on your grind, son. Let's get this money and take over Harlem in the process."

Wetto took the book bag off of his shoulder and filled it with the kilos before tossing it to one of his young Bloods. "Yo, I'll never forget this look out, kid. I know my brother, Peetho, looking down from heaven with a big smile on his face. Growing up, he'd always told me how one hunnit you were.

I guessed y'all hit a few licks together or whatever and you had his back when the heat was on. I wished you'd a been there when them cops caught him slipping at the bodega on Thirteenth Ave last summer. Maybe he'd still be here right now." He lowered his head, then jumped up and shook up with me.

"No doubt had I been there, I'd a bussed my gun until it was empty. Your brother was a good dude, but God got him now."

Wetto nodded. "It's all love. Blood out, my nigga. One."

Eve got up and closed the door behind them. She locked it and kicked off her Jordans. She walked across the carpet on pink socks. "Yo, how the fuck did you get that nigga Wetto to agree to get down with you? All of   these so called hittas around here fear that young nigga. He can be our gold mine." She sat on my lap and laid her cheek against mine.

I placed my hand on the bottom of her ass and rubbed it from there on to her thick thighs that was encased in some tight Fendi jeans. "You know me and his brother Peetho used to hit licks together back when I was in middle school. That was before you hopped off the stoop. We used to highjack niggas for their foreign rides and sell them to the Dino's Chop Shop where he'd give us like five gees a piece for each. Seven if the engine was semi new.

Anyway, when I first became a Blood, that fool Peetho was with me. We got initiated at the same time. Part of our initiation was that we had to smoke two Crip niggas out in the Bronx. Long story short, on the night we smashed out there, this nigga Peetho was so hyped on the Oxys and Xans, he refused to put his mask on.

We rolled up on two Crip niggas as they were coming out of a barbecue joint. I jumped out of the passenger's seat, ran right up to one of them, and put three in his face, snatching the blue rag from around his neck and sopping it with his blood. Before I turned to run away, I threw a red rag on his chest.

Peetho chased down the other nigga and popped him twice before his gun jammed. But the nigga wound up jumping from the concrete and running away. When Peetho got back in the car, he made it seem like everything was cool. I didn't find out what happened until a week later.

I was once again chilling with him and we were scoping the boulevard, looking for a nigga's ride to jack. Well, all that came to a halt when two blue

Chevys rolled up on our van. Four niggas got out of the car with their pistols out and blue rags around their necks.

Before I could get my pistol off of my hip, they lit our whip up. They rocked that bitch for thirty seconds straight and I got caught with three of the slugs. One here." I pointed to my shoulder. "Another here."

I pointed to my right rib cage. "And one of the bullets got stuck here." I pointed to my hipbone. "This nigga didn't catch a slug, but while he was driving me to the hospital, he told me everything. He confirmed the first nigga that jumped out of the Chevy was the one that he should have killed and would have, if his gun didn't jam. I was furious. I'd never forgiven him for that shit.

I had plans on getting out of the hospital and smoking his ass, but if you can remember, they wound up taking me to juvenile hall for like three months because I had all of those warrants. After I got out, he caught an adult case and did six years in prison. Came out and made two kids and got married.

The first time I ran into him was last summer. I caught his ass coming out of the bodega down the way and made him eat my slugs. I'm the one that slumped his ass. Finally got my revenge and it felt so fucking good. However, all of the time we were hustling, he talked about how much heart his little brother Wetto had.

How he was from the motherland and out there in Havana raising hell. I'd never got a chance to meet lil' homey until a few months ago. I confirmed what he'd always told me not only by sight, but also by the word of the slums. Nah'mean?"

Eve stood up and placed both legs over my lap before sitting back down, looking me in the eyes. "You're a dirty muthafucka. And I be wondering why I'm so fucking heartless. It's because I've come up under you. Damn." She shook her head and ran her finger over my lips. "You kilt that nigga's brother and you got his ass working for you. He's about to sew up all of Harlem on your half and you don't see nothing wrong with that, do you?" She held the sides of my face and looked into my eyes.

"Hell n'all, I don't. As far as I'm concerned, I'm throwing his brother a bone. Somebody oughta be thanking me. I'ma let that nigga get a nice amount of paper, then when I feel like he gettin' too big, I'ma have to knock him down a few pegs. Ain't no nigga fit to be King other than me, nah'mean?" I sucked her lips into my mouth and wrestled with her tongue. We breathed heavily into each other's mouths. I could feel my dick throbbing under the weight of her ass in my lap.

"Damn, Showbiz. I swear to God, don't no nigga drive me as crazy as you do. You just got that real gutter and grimy shit in you and I be wanting you to put it as far into me as you can." She rolled her back and sucked on my neck. "You lucky I gotta go pick my aunt up from the airport, or I'd have to get me some of that big ass dick, the long way." She kissed my lips and hopped up with her nipples sticking through her shirt.

After she left, I sat there on the couch trying to see what she saw. In my opinion, I wasn't shiesty at all. I was surviving in the slums of New York where not even the strongest survived.

Chapter 8

It took six months for me to break into Spanish Harlem the right way. My uncle Javier had started out sending me a base of twenty kilos a month. By the third month after I put Wetto down with me, I was moving twenty kilos every ten days. That meant a minimum of sixty a month at fifty gees profit for each one. That was three million a month. I was finally able to peek into the life I wanted to live. I started out by forcing the three Arab owners of the bodegas on Tenth, Eleventh, and Twelfth Avenue to give me their businesses.

My young Bloods rose hell two weeks straight, going inside of the stores and ransacking them as they shouted, "This property belongs to Showbiz." The owners then got the message and I was able to buy them out at $50,000 in cash. As soon as they left, I allowed Eve to fill those slots, which she did with a few of the business-minded sistas from our hood. She started taking classes online to obtain her business degree. I didn't have no time nor the patience for that shit, so I let her handle all of the book smart aspects of things.

I was on my goon shit. I took to shaking down the businesses around our projects. If they weren't from our community, then they were forced out or they had to pay me and the Bloods a hefty protection fee of twenty gees a week. If the end of the week came and I didn't have that cash in hand, then their businesses were fucked up and often set ablaze. I wasn't playing. My goal was to conquer my entire hood first. Then I would venture out into the Black part of Harlem where it was going to be a little more difficult to make niggas honor my gangsta.

It took another four months for me to fully get a firm grasp on Spanish Harlem. In order for me to do that, I had to throw a major feast that cost me $15,000 for all of the Bloods in my hood. I held it at the Harlem River Park. Eve got all of the Puerto Rican, Dominican, West Indies, and Cuban women to come out and tend to the barbecue grills, bringing a dish from their homes to feed us Bloods with. They had about ten grills smoking. I watched Eve walk around and stand on the women with an iron fist. She told them to make sure that none of us were without a full plate or glass in front of us at all times.

I sat in the distance on top of a picnic table next to Wetto. I bit into a Brat and chewed with a smile on my face as I watched my niggas being attended to by some of the baddest bitches in New York City. These women had on real small booty shorts that were all up their asses. Their long hair fell past their waist. Their tops were so short that they showed off their sexy stomachs. Kids ran all around chasing one another, while others sat at their tables stuffing their faces. Some of them played basketball on the courts.

Across from them, close to the parking lot, were about twenty little girls jumping rope. While they waited for their turn to jump, they licked on ice cream cones, laughed, and joked with one another. There were little boys out chasing a bunch of girls with super soaker water guns. The girls would scream and take off running. Everywhere I looked, there was a Blood nigga on security looking for predators. I nodded my head. I was starting to feel like a king in my own right.

Wetto bit into his barbecued hamburger and chased it with some plain potato chips. He chewed it with his mouth open and sipped out of the twenty-ounce bottle of orange Faygo soda pop. "All my niggas eating like never before, Showbiz. I just wanna let you know that we love you, kid, and if ever it come down to it, we'll burn this city down at your command. That's my word." He wiped his hand on a napkin and then his mouth.

"The best is yet to come, Blood. Now that we got Spanish Harlem on lock, I say we venture out and fuck with the Black side of town. Get them niggas to fuck with us. What Blood n'em talking about out there?" I asked, biting into my Brat. The juice popped into my mouth and I had to close my eyes for a second because it was so good.

"My fam ready to have a sit down with you. He say he like how you handling shit over here. He got about a hunnit niggas that's behind him. He running Harlem right now and he looking for a new plug. If you wanna fuck with him, I can guarantee you'll gross the same type of numbers you are out here. He's a good nigga. All about his paper. Real loyal to the Blood line, too."

I drank a quarter of my grape pop and burped into my fist as I watched Eve move around the gathering, giving orders to the ladies in her Burberry dress. It was so tight, I could literally make out the crack of her ass under it. I shook my head. "Nah, son. You remember what I told you. I'm only fucking with you. If you think that'll be a good fit, I'ma put the dope in your hands. You can fuck with him all you want, just as long as those numbers add up. Nah'mean?"

I knew I could have taken the initiative and sat down with Kam and tried to lock shit up that way, but I didn't want to go that route. I wanted everything to flow through Wetto because he had so much pull. I didn't know that nigga Kam from Adam. So he would have no loyalty to me but when it came to his blood, Wetto, the love was there.

Not only would Wetto be putting him on to some top-notch heroin, but he'd be helping him to fully conquer his portion of Harlem. Together, they would own the entire Harlem. I just wanted to sit at the top of the throne and let them do all of the work.

Wetto nodded his head. "I'ma fuck with him 'cause I know he a good nigga. He's half Cuban, so that real shit is in his blood. I'll have a sit down with him early in the morning. You just be ready for me to cop another fifty kilos, ASAP. The Vegas gotta be eating like crazy off of Harlem," he said, laughing.

"We doing alright but ain't near where we wanna be just yet." I looked around at all of my people with a grin on my face.

Wetto took a long swallow from his soda pop and wiped his mouth. "Yeah, well like I said, if it ever comes down to it, all you need to know is that you got a bunch of hungry killers riding behind you. Every muhfucka out here know who's the one making sure their shorties are fed every night. It ain't no secret, big homey. I got a lot of love for you, kid. Word up." He grabbed my hand and gave me a half hug.

I pat his back and embraced him. "That's good to know, lil' bruh. Keep doing ya thing. I'll make sure that you're straight on a regular. That's my word."

Instead of waiting until the following morning, Wetto strolled out to the black side of Harlem and had a sit down with Kam that same night. I got a call the first thing in the morning for fifty kilos as promised. After I hung up with them, I called up my uncle Javier, and the shipment was in route all the way from Havana.

* * *

A month after that event, I copped myself a nice lil' spot in upper Manhattan, right outside of Spanish Harlem. The crib was in a low key Dominican section. It had three bedrooms and a bathroom and a half. Real spacious and the best part was that I actually had grass around my brownstone.

Growing up in the slums of Spanish Harlem, most would tell you that seeing somebody with grass was rare. First off, there weren't many places for it to grow and secondly, if it did, people took to walking on it as if it was a doormat. So, the fact that I had some was cool as hell to me. I had a mind to water it every day.

On the second to last day before moving out of my old crib, Tori showed up with Maine in her arms. He was sleeping as she walked through the doorway with a big smile on her face. "I see on Facebook that you're moving. Damn, you weren't about to call and let nobody know." She stopped in the doorway and looked me up and down before stepping inside and laying him on the bed in the master bedroom. She came out of there and placed her hand on her hip. "Well?"

I was high as fuck. It took me a few minutes to even register what she was talking about. I closed the door and locked it, then ran my fingers through my hair, which was all over the place. I'd just woke up from a two-hour slumber. As soon as my eyes popped open, I got my nose together. I was beaming.

"Yeah, I'm just moving to upper Manhattan. I'm tired of staying in the same hood that I'm serving my weight in. A real hustler knows that you're never supposed to shit where you sleep. Nah'mean?"

She smirked. "Yeah right. You just trying to get away from everybody. Now that you having all this money, I can tell that mad people been hitting you up left and right. Shit, it's hard out here and I don't blame 'em." She walked over to the couch and sat on it, crossing her thighs. The Nine West skirt rose and exposed more of her caramel skin.

I sat on the love seat across from her, just drinking her body in. She was so small, yet at the same time, she was strapped and fine as a muthafucka. I didn't give a fuck that she was my baby mother's sister. I'd always found her very attractive and alluring. "Yo, Tori. Why did you really come over here? I know it ain't got nothing to do with me leaving. Do it?" I asked, peering at her thighs again. I wanted her to open them.

From where I was sitting, had she opened them, I would have been able to see all up her skirt. I was banking on her pussy being as fat as her sister's. I wanted to know what it felt like, if she could handle my dick or would she beg me to take it easy like Punkin used to. I looked into her pretty face.

She smacked her lips. "That is the reason I came over here. I also wanted you to spend some time with your son. He's been saying Da-Da a lot, so I'm guessing it's time for y'all to get to know each other, even though Ebony ain't trying to make the effort. But you know how she is." She uncrossed her thighs and I saw a hint of her pink panties. I felt a shiver go down my spine, and my dick began to harden.

Ever since Tori had come into New York, she and I had not really developed a strong relationship. Every time she was around Punkin and I, all we did was argue and fight like cats and dogs. She'd often be in the middle, trying to break things up between us. I was never able to really gauge how she felt about me and never asked.

I got up and slid beside her on the couch, placing my arm around the back of it, looking down on her. She smelled like Cherry Blossom perfume. It mixed nicely with her natural essence. I looked down at her thick thighs and shuddered once again. "Yo, anybody ever tell you that you're bad as fuck? Huh?"

She jerked her head back and looked at me from the corner of her eyes. "What?"

"You heard me. Have anybody ever told you how bad you are?"

She stood up and looked down on me with a crazy look on her face. "Okay, maybe this was a bad idea. I shouldn't have come. Let me go in here and get Maine and I'll be on my way." She pulled her skirt down and was about to make her way out of the living room when I grabbed her wrist.

"Shorty, calm yo' ass down. Come here. " I yanked her, causing her to fall on to my lap. Her big ass fit perfectly on my crotch. She tried to get up again, but I pulled her back down. "Stop playing wit' me, Tori, and stay yo' ass right here. Damn."

"I ain't finna stay on yo' fucking lap. You're my sister's baby daddy. What the fuck I look like, Showbiz?" She tried to get up, but I kept my big arm wrapped around her small waist. She struggled against me and after seeing I wasn't about to let her go, she surrendered and sighed out loud.

"Damn, man. What do you want?" She rolled her eyes and looked into mine.

"Yo, what kind of car you rolling out there?" I asked, touching her chin with my forefinger and thumb.

She smacked my hand away. "I ain't got no car yet. I just told you it was hard out there. Me and your son rode the subway, followed by the bus. That's how we got here."

I shook my head and looked down at her thick thighs again. Her skirt had risen a lot more, nearly to her crotch because of all of the struggling between us. I placed my hand on them. "You way too bad to be on the fucking train or a bus. How about I take you down to the car lot in the morning and let you roll off that bitch with something fresh? Put yo' name on the paperwork and everything. What'll you say?" I asked, sliding my hand in between her thighs and forcing them slightly apart.

She arched her back and bit into her bottom lip. "Damn, Showbiz. That's how you gon' play shit? Why you just can't look out for me because I'm your son's aunt?" She took a hold of my hand and moved it off of her. "I ain't going. I love my sister way too much to cross her by fucking with you."

I grabbed her hair and yanked her head backward. "Then how about I take this pussy and we still go and get you a Benz off of the lot tomorrow morning? After I wear this ass out all night." My dick was throbbing like crazy. The way I had her head pulled back, made her open her thighs wide.

Her skirt rose and revealed her pussy-packed, pink lace panties. I slid my hand in between them and rubbed a finger up and down where her lips were pressing up against the material. The cloth sunk further into her gap. I could feel the heat on my finger. I sucked on her neck and scraped at it with my teeth.

"What's it gone be, Tori?"

"Uh, stop. Get away from me. I ain't going. I already told you what it is." She hit my wrist and tried to hop off of my lap.

I pulled her back down and wormed two fingers into the leg hole of her panties. Her lips were hot and fleshy. I searched for her opening and after a few seconds, I found it. I slid my two fingers all the way up her box and got to working them in and out swiftly.

She opened her thighs wide and closed her eyes. Her hips involuntarily bucked forward into my fingers, driving them deep into her box. She tried to grab at my wrist again, but I could tell that her willpower was leaving her.

"Get yo' fingers out of there. You so bogus. Shit!"

She scrunched her face and threw her head backward. I fingered her as fast as I could, watching them go in and out of her meaty pussy. The crotch band of her panties was on the back of my hand as I worked that cat like crazy. Her pussy started to get wet and juices oozed out of her. I sucked my fingers into my mouth, picked her up, and fell to the floor with her.

"Take these muhfucking panties off right now!" I pulled and ripped them from her frame.

"Aw, fuck. Don't do this, Showbiz. Please, I can't fuck my sister's baby daddy. Please, Showbiz!"

I pulled my shorts down and then my boxers. My dick was standing tall against my stomach, throbbing like crazy as I got between her legs and ran my big head up and down her slit. Her essence was pouring out of her like a dam.

I leaned down and sucked on her neck, positioned my dick and stabbed it home, going deep into her womb. She bucked her hips and squeezed her eyelids tighter. "Aw shit, Showbiz. You're in me now. You're in me. You so bogus. You so fucking bogus! Aww!" she moaned and bit into her bottom lip with her eyes closed.

I slid my hand under her shoulder, forcing her into a ball as I worked my dick in and out of her sopping wet cat. Every time I pulled my dick back, her walls sucked at me. They seemed to beg me to slam it home as hard as I could. So, that's what I did. I got to long stroking that forbidden pussy as hard as I could while sucking all over her neck. Her feet bounced up and down while on my shoulders.

Bam. Bam. Bam. Bam.

That was the sound of our skin slapping into each other as I attacked that pussy. "You know you wanted this dick! Tell me, Tori! Tell me you love this dick!" I growled, fucking her harder. She opened her eyes and I saw them roll into the back of her head. Her tongue ran all over her lips.

"Damn. Damn. Slow down. Fuck. You murking my pussy. You killing me." She stuck her nails into my lower back and drug them across my skin. I could feel the stinging as they traveled across me. "Un. Un. Ooohh, shit! Slow down. Slow down," she whimpered.

I stopped with my dick lodged deep within her, ripped her shirt down the middle and then pulled her bra off of her. I had always found Tori to be so fucking cold. Even when me and Punkin were together, I always told myself that one day I would get her pussy. I felt if I could fuck her one time, she'd never leave my side. Not that I wanted her to be my woman or nothing but having another dime in the stable couldn't hurt.

She opened her thighs wide and gripped my waist as I pounded into her. "You're killing me, Showbiz. Aw, shit. You're so deep. Don't cum in me!" she screamed, then sucked all over my lips.

I pushed her ass backward so I could see her big titties bounce up and down while I piped her. They wobbled on her chest with their erect nipples that looked like big Hershey Kisses. I licked all over her areola and pulled on each one with my teeth, before sucking the nipple into my mouth.

My dick was like a battering ram. My hips were working over time to give me the motion to go as deep and as fast as I could. She reached between her legs and tweaked her clit, then sucked her fingers into her mouth. Her eyes rolled into the back of her head. She sat all the way up as I continued to kill her.

"Aww! Aww! Aww! Showbiz! You dirty mutha-fuckal I'm cumming. I'm cumming so hard!" she screamed and wrapped her little arms around my neck while she seemed to have a seizure.

I rolled my thumb around her clit as I stroked and stroked. I was seconds away from cumming. I watched her big titties bounce. She took a hold of them and pushed them together and it became too much of a sight for me. I came deep within her channel, jerking like crazy.

Her pussy was twice as good as Punkin's had ever been, tighter and wetter. It felt like she had scales on the inside. I wasn't trying to let that be the last and only time I fucked. I needed her to be my in house pussy.

After I pulled out, she scooted away from me and put her back up against the couch. She brought her knees to her chest and sat her chin on top of them. "You ain't right, Showbiz. I can't believe you just did that." She looked over to me and shook her head.

I crawled over and sat beside her. My dick was still sticking straight up in the air. I put my arm around her shoulder. "Yo, this what it's gon' be. From here on out, I'ma make sure you're straight. You gon' be my lil' boo thang. I'ma keep you in the crib but anything you need, I'ma make sure you got it. I was feeling you even when Punkin was alive. Let me just throw that out there right now. She gon', so I gotta have you. It's as simple as that."

I kissed her on the cheek and stood up. She slowly made her way to her feet. She lowered her head. "But that was my big sister, though. I would never feel right being with you knowing that you're her ex. I don't think I would be able to live with myself." She stepped into her torn panties, then saw that they were pointless to try and put on, simply pulling her skirt down. Her pussy was puffy. The lips slightly open. I thought that shit looked hot.

I grabbed her by the arms and slammed her against the wall, looking into her brown eyes. "Yo, I don't know what's giving you the impression that you have a choice because you don't. What I want, I get and I gotta have you. I don't give a fuck what you or nobody else gotta say about it. Let me upgrade you, shorty, because whatever you been doing ain't working. You belong to me now. You understand that?"

She swallowed and nodded her head. "Yes, but what about Ebony and the rest of my family? They gone disown me once they find out that we're fucking around. Don't you think so?"

I shrugged my shoulders. "Fuck 'em. You're a big girl now. You belong to me. I got you. I'll be all the family you'll ever need." I kissed her on the lips and cuffed her ass through her skirt. I trailed my tongue all over them. "Kiss me and let's make this shit official. That's all you gotta do. Kiss me if you want me like I want you." I licked her lips. She tilted her head back and closed her eyes.

She sighed and opened them. "You promise you'll never leave me in the dust, Showbiz?" I nodded. "That's my word, shorty. Just kiss my lips. Okay?" She wrapped her arms around my neck and kissed my lips with tears running down her cheeks.

"They gon' hate my guts, Showbiz." She kissed my lips and sucked them into her mouth.

"Fuck 'em. You riding wit' me now."

Chapter 9

As expected, Tori's family turned their backs on her the moment they found out that her and I were fucking around. Her sister Ebony was the first person she'd exposed it to and it didn't take her more than an hour to get the word out to their entire family and some of their friends. Even some of her cousins tried to jump her. It was crazy, but she was forced to stand as a woman and give them the finger.

I mean I don't really know why I wanted her so bad. I think I was just one of those rotten niggas in general. I loved to go against the grain. I was my own man and liked to cause a stir. Tori had been the only one in their family that tried to keep my son in my life, even when her sister Ebony was throwing a lot of shade. So, on the one hand, I respected and commended her for standing her ground and doing what was right. That was until I forced her to follow me and do what was wrong.

The day I took the pussy from her, she'd traveled to my crib by Subway and a fucking bus. The next morning, I took her to a Mercedes Benz lot and bought her a newly released Benz truck fresh off of the showroom floor. I gave her the keys and the title and paid for her insurance. Then I took her on a shopping spree down on Fifth Avenue and spent twenty bands on her just for the sport.

I wasn't feeling her simple wardrobe, so I had to make sure she was brought up to my standards. How the fuck was I gon' have a bad bitch lying around my crib who wasn't even up to my standards? That wasn't possible. I was Showbiz.

After we got her wardrobe up to par, next came her hair and nails. I gave her the rest of the day for her beauty treatments, then the next day we signed her up for college courses. I wanted her to specifically take business management and finances courses. That way she could teach me the legal and educational side of things. I was taking over businesses and placing them in the hangs of females Eve was putting in place.

I needed to know how to look over their shoulders and understand how to advance the businesses. I wasn't quite sure where I wanted to go with them one hundred percent, but I understood that educating myself was the first step no matter where I wanted to go.

Eve came to me about three months after me and Tori had been fucking around. We were having my son's second birthday party, waiting for Ebony to show up with him when Eve grabbed me by my shirt as I walked past her in the hallway.

She pulled me toward the bathroom and I smacked her hand away, mugging her lil' ass. "What the fuck is you doing?" I asked with about five balloons in my hand that I was about to tape to the wall of my living room.

She mugged me and pointed toward the bathroom. "Let me holler at you for a minute, kid." She stepped inside first and waited for me to step through before she closed the door. I thought she was on some freaky shit.

Even though Tori was at the party, had Eve wanted to get down, I would have picked her lil' ass up and fucked her against the wall like it was the most natural thing in the world. Her pussy was that good. "Yo, what's good, ma? Why you looking all angry and shit?"

She pinched her nose and sucked her teeth loudly. "On my word, Showbiz, if you wasn't my big homey, I'd put two in yo' melon, son. Word is bond." She mugged me with more anger than I've ever seen in her eyes before. I was confused. I started to replay everything that I'd done over the last few weeks that could have pissed her off. I knew I was making sure we were bringing in bag loads of money.

Harlem was juking all across the board, both on the black and Spanish sides. It was to the point that I was sending my uncle Javier three million dollars in cash a month just to re-up with the Vega's heroin. I'd gotten a few orders for cocaine from the Bloods on the West side of Harlem around this time.

I was thinking of investing five hundred thousand towards that so we could really eat, so I was confused. In my head, I was doing every thing the right way. "What the fuck are you talking about, Evelina?"

"Nigga, you been fucking with that Tori bitch for months now? When was you gon' tell me this shit?" she asked, frowning. I smacked my lips and looked down on her as if she'd lost her mind.

"Man, you sweating me over fucking wit' a bitch? I'm thinking I did something else. I ain't think it was that important. Why you acting like you salty and shit?" It wasn't like Eve to get all in her chest about me fucking with a female.

Like I said before, her and I were just cool. We'd tried the whole dating thing when we were kids and it hadn't worked out. She knew I loved pussy too much even though she was bad and all of that shit. Whenever I saw another chick equal to her beauty, I wanted to know what her pussy felt like.

I wanted to know how she got down in the bedroom. The noises she made when I stroked her as deep as I could. What she smelled like. I was one of them type of niggas. Always had been. I didn't even think being in love with a woman could stop me from wanting to fuck other bitches. Pussy was just too good. I was a feen for it.

"Showbiz, you already know how I am when it comes to you. I know you ain't my nigga or nothing like that but at the same time, I don't like no bitch impeding on my territory without me knowing about it. Like it or not, you and I fuck from time to time which means I should at least know who you putting that pipe to. It's way too many diseases out here for me not to know. Then, out of all bitches, you gotta fuck wit' Punkin's sister. What the fuck are you on?" She had a distasteful look with her face. I sat on the rim of the sink and looked down on her.

"Eve, yo. You bugging right now. I don't jock you for them lil' bitches that you be fucking from time to time. That shit ain't my bitness. I can't control you, just like you can't control me. Let's get that straight out the gate. Secondly, Tori is clean. She's my in-house pussy. Every rich nigga need one. I was feeling shorty even when her sister was alive. I had to have her, so this is what it is. Me and you ain't fucked in months anyway. I know you ain't been on no celibate shit, right?"

"That ain't the point, Showbiz. You already know that I'd never keep shit from you. I been around you and this bitch for the last three months and ain't nobody told me shit. I don't like when you be fucking wit' hoes that be all in my face and it's more than what I'm thinking. Me and you ain't supposed to keep shit from one another. You're my heart, Show-biz and you know that." She stepped in front of me, laying her head on my chest. I rubbed her back and exhaled loudly.

"Damn, Eve. Yo, I ain't know that it was that serious. You know I don't give a fuck about nobody more than I care about you. After my mother, you're my number one. I'd murder a nigga or a bitch over you. I love you with all of my cold ass heart. You're my rider."

"I know that, Showbiz. So, why you just can't fuck these hoes and leave it at that? Why these bitches gotta have titles and shit? Especially when you already know they ain't gon' ride for you when the heat is on. The only bitch that's gone buss her gun for you is me. I never liked that bitch Punkin. I was low key glad when she finally kicked the bucket. I felt like there were no more threats around. Now here comes this bitch. The same blood line and everything. I can only imagine what she thinking in her head." She took a step back and pulled her .9 millimeter out of the small of her back and cocked it. "On every thing, I should go out there and buck this bitch because I ain't going. You only got one woman that stand beside me and you and that's me." She curled her lip.

Her chest heaved up and down. I could tell she was excited. I frowned and stepped forward, holding her face in my hands.

"Eve, look at me," I demanded. She continued to look at the ground, and then very slowly, her eyes trailed up to meet mine.

"What, Juanito?"

"Ma, you acting like you wanna fuck wit' me on that level again. I have never seen you this heated over me fucking off wit' a bitch. What's really good?" She shook her head. "Nothing. I already told you. I just don't like bitches thinking they got stakes in your franchise. I buss my gun for you. I don't give a fuck who you fucking but once they get titles, staying all in your crib and shit, walking around this muhfucka like they own it, then I get vexed. I'm the only Queen. Point blank, period."

All of the sudden, the bathroom felt like it was a million degrees. I had a trace of sweat on my forehead and needed to get some fresh air. I didn't understand where she was coming from, but I knew it was in my best interest to respect it and try to calm her down or I saw her going out there and putting a clip full of bullets into Tori's head.

Had that happened, I wouldn't have stopped her. I cared about Tori and I knew I would protect her from harm or anybody else, except when it came to Eve. If Eve wanted to kill her, as crazy as it sounds and if I couldn't talk her out of it, I would have wound up chopping Tori's body up along side of her. That would have sucked, because I honestly cared about her to a certain extent. I kissed her on the forehead.

"Put that banger up, ma. That shit ain't even worth it. You already know what it is. I only got one Queen and that Queen is you. Just like you only got one King." I kissed her juicy lips and rubbed my cheek against hers.

"See, that's what I'm saying, Showbiz. I don't want you doing all that lovey dovey shit with these hoes that you do to me. They don't deserve that love and respect. Only I do." She fixed her .9 and placed it back into the small of her back.

"Yo, I get it and you're right. I gotta work on that. But for now, what do you say about me and you just going out and kicking it tonight? Let's hit up Cheeks strip club and get one of them bitches to treat us right. Maybe we just need to spend some time together outside of this hustling shit. I think we losing sight of who we are to each other. At least you are," I teased her and nudged her with my elbow.

She smirked and sucked her teeth. "Oh, its just me, huh? Let you find out that I'd been fucking with another nigga for three months on some in-house shit without telling you. Nigga, you'd probably knock that nigga's head off and then fuck me up so bad, they have to take me to Urgent Care. So you're getting off easy right now. Don't get shit twisted. Just because you ain't technically my nigga and I ain't your woman, don't mean shit sweet. Come on now. You better let Tori know what it is ASAP. It's the only way she gon' keep some air in her lungs. Word is bond, B."

She kissed my lips. "That outing sounds like a good idea, too. I think I need to let loose for a night. Then my uncle wants us to take care of some more bitness. He say we can make up to sixty gees depending on how we handle things. Either way, I need you by my side or is the dope money changing that killer shit in you?"

I wrapped my arm around her waist and pulled her to me. Kissing her soft lips, I rubbed all over that big ass booty. "Never that. I live to kill and kill to live. Blood Gang to the death of me. Never forget that." She grabbed the back of my head and slid her tongue into my mouth, sucking my lips while moaning deep within her throat.

* * *

Later that night, we stepped into the club, Cheeks. I was Gucci down from my shoulders to socks. My boxers were even Gucci. The fit was majority black with specks of red Gucci symbols all over the shirt and pants. Hanging out my right pocket just a tad was my red rag. I had a bottle of Moet in one hand and Patron in the other.

Before we'd stepped into the club, I'd tooted a gram of heroin. I was lifted. Eve had on a black and red Gucci skirt dress that stopped at the bottom of her ass cheeks. Her all jet-black stockings had specks of red Gucci symbols going through them. On her feet were some red bottom Balenciaga's.

Her long curly hair flowed down her back. She had her edges on fleek and a red rag tied tightly around her right wrist. Before I was able to size up the other bitches in the club, I was convinced that she had all they ass on smash. She was the epitome of a bad bitch. I slid my arm around her slid waist as we stepped into the dark club. It smelled like weed smoke, perfume, sweat and cigarettes in the air. I inhaled deeply and smiled. I was ready to turn the fuck up. "Yo, let's buss this bitch open, ma."

She smiled with her eyes lowered into slits and held up her bottle of Moet. "Let's get it." We stepped past the coat checks and was met by a thick ass red bone with tattoos all over her body. She had blue hair and a purple and black Victoria Secret's bikini panty and bra set on.

The panties were pulled up so far, I could make out both of her pussy lips. "May I ask you two what kind of evening you're looking forward to having tonight?" She looked me up and down and licked her lips. She had a gold ball in the middle of her tongue. Eve must of peeped her, stepping in front of me and backing her big ass into my front.

"We are looking to make it rain in this bitch. Give us two of your baddest bitches and point us to your most expensive private room. Make sure the bitches eat pussy, too. I'm trying to enjoy myself. Word is bond." There were three different stages in the lower portion of Cheeks and another on the second level of the club.

All three stages had dancers on them. I looked over the redbone's shoulder and saw one with two Spanish looking hoes with their asses up against one another's, twerking to Drake's "Nice for What" track. Their titties shook on their chest as they got it in.

"I'm sorry, ma'am, but we don't do that kind of thing here. Our club is very professional and by the book. I can point you to a private room, but I assure you that nothing like that will take place." Eve frowned, stepped forward, and grabbed a handful of the red bone's hair, before tonguing her ass down and rubbing all over her booty.

After she broke the kiss, she stood back, reached into her Gucci handbag, and grabbed ten thousand dollars worth of ones. She took a nice portion of it and tossed it into her face. "Bitch, Gang-Gang in the building. Now point us to the best room you got. Snatch up another bitch and bring yo' ass wit' her. I like how you taste. " She wiped the red bone's lips and smiled. My dick was so hard because of how gangsta she was, that I wanted to fuck her right there in front of the whole club, and it was packed.

* * *

Eve leaned across the table and kissed my lips, before sitting back on the couch as the red bone opened her legs and sat her big ass between them. She placed her hands on her knees and rubbed her booty up and down Eve's slit, looking back at her. "You like that, mama?" the stripped asked.

Eve pulled her skirt dress all the way up. She didn't have no panties on. She held her sex lips open while the red bone did her thing. "Hell yeah, bitch. Pop that ass a lil' more. Hit my jewel with that big thang before you eat it." She fanned about a hundred dollars in ones over her head and opened her thighs wider.

I had a strapped ass caramel chick in my lap. She was short and thick as hell. I slid a condom down my dick and made her sit on that muhfucka while I watched Eve and the red bone do their thing. Her pussy sucked at my pipe. She'd bend all the way over and then sit down on my tool. The shit felt so good. I smacked her big ass.

"Ride this dick. Earn that money, shorty. I know you got bills and shit." I laughed and dropped two thousand in ones in front of her. "Aww damn, daddy. Yo' shit so long and thick," she groaned, sliding up and down it. I watched Eve put her knees on the couch and bend all the way over. She held her ass cheeks apart.

"Bitch, eat all this shit. Earn these dollars." She reached under herself and opened her pussy for the red bone. The red bone got on her knees and stuck her face into Eve's playground. She licked up and down it and sucked on her pussy lips one at a time, causing her to moan at the top of her lungs.

I noted that the red bone's thong was in between her pussy lips. Both of her yellow lips were exposed. The crinkle of her ass hole winked at me. I got to murdering the caramel bitch on my lap. I was fucking her so hard, the side of her face was sliding along the table. "Uh. Uh. Uh. Uh. Uh. Holy Shit. Holy Shit. Holy Shit. Uh. Aww, shit!" she hollered, beating on the table top with her balled fist.

Drool leaked out of the corner of her mouth. She closed her eyes and smiled as I kilt that ass. The red bone drove her tongue in and out of Eve's hole. She sucked her asshole and fingered her with two digits at full speed.

The red bone's ass cheeks shook as she did her thing. I watched her slide her fingers under herself as she played with her own pussy. I'd had all I could take. I felt the caramel bitch nutting all over my dick.

I pushed her ass on the table and threw a bundle of ones in her face before moving her out of my way.

I climbed across the table and pulled the red bone's thong to the side, exposing her chubby pussy with lips that looked swollen and ready for a hard dicking. She looked over her shoulder at me and flicked her tongue at me. "Come get this shit, nigga!" I slapped that ass and grabbed her hair, forcing her face back into Eve's slit before I took my head and slammed my dick home into her furnace. Her ass cheeks crashed into my waist.

"Shit! His dick huge!" she moaned. I grabbed two handfuls of her ass and got to working her over. The caramel bitch came over and bit into my back. She sucked all over my neck and jiggled my balls.

"He finna stretch yo' shit open, Pox. My shit killing me right now, but it felt so good." She knelt on the couch and helped the red bone eat Eve's pussy. They kissed and sucked over each other's faces. I had three fat ass booties bent over in front of me.

I can't even describe how that made me feel. All I know is that I got to fucking the red bone so hard, she stopped eating Eve's pussy and began moaning and screaming like I was torturing her. Her box was a real tight fit like she ain't have that many miles on it. That shit made me kill it even more. I was even laughing at my own sadistic shit.

Eve flipped over and sat on the couch. She wrapped her thick thighs over the caramel bitch's head and got to ride her face from her back. "Fuck that bitch, Showbiz. Gang-Gang that bitch," she moaned. She humped faster and faster. Her mouth opened wide. "Shit, this bitch made me cum. She made me cum, Blood! Aww, fuck!" she groaned and got to shuddering.

I pulled out of the red bone bitch and took my rubber off. Moved both her and the caramel chick out of the way and got between Eve's legs, sliding right into her wet box. With long hard strokes, I was trying to plant her into the couch.

Bam! Bam! Bam! Bam!

I kissed all over her lips. "This my pussy. You know this my pussy, Eve!" I snapped, biting on her neck.

"Uh! Juanito! Okay, daddy. Okay! Shit!"

She pulled me down and licked all over my face, breathing heavily. I squeezed her titties through the dress, fucking her like a stallion. Damn, the pussy was too good. Before I knew it, a few more strokes and I was releasing my seed deep within her channel.

"Shit. I love you so much!" she cried out in ecstasy as her body convulsed, dragging her nails across my back.

* * *

After we left the club and before I pulled out of the parking lot that night, I asked Eve how she found out about me and Tori. She said that Ebony had told her. I filed that away. I was going to use that revelation as motivation to fuck Ebony over down the road somewhere.

Chapter 10

I flipped my black hoodie over my head and wiggled my fingers into the black gloves. The rain began to beat against the windshield of the Toyota Four Runner I'd stolen so Eve and I could hit a lick for Veeto. It was worth eighty thousand dollars. I sat in the driver's seat of the truck high as a kite. I'd put a half gram up each nostril and popped two Percocet sixties. I was fucked up but on point. I was ready to kill something. With that heroin in my system, I felt invincible.

Eve pulled her gloves over her hands and sniffed. She wiped her mouth and looked over to me with a mug on her pretty face. "Yo, we gotta make sure we fuck this family over, Showbiz. This fuck nigga is supposed to be in the witness protection program. He's set to go before the grand jury in two weeks. His testimony can bring down the entire Cali Cartel.

It's our job to not let that happen. Veeto said he want everybody in the house killed so sadistically, it will send a message that his hit men are the best in all of the United States. That's why I'm bringing these along." She pulled up her hoodie and showed me the knives that were all around her waist in their holsters.

"Yo, let me get one of them bitches. I'm trying to slice some shit up, too." I grabbed one of the knives off of her waist and put it on mine.

"Just let me handle the kids, Showbiz. I don't know how you feel about slumping a shorty, but I don't give a fuck. You ready to go?" She placed her hand on the door handle.

I nodded and kissed her lips. "A'ight, let's handle this bitness, ma. Time is money."

I stepped out into the night with the rain coming down like pelts. The wind howled. Thunder roared in the sky before a lightning bolt flashed across it, illuminating the gated community. Veeto had the guard on his payroll, so there wasn't any problem rolling past his post and up the winding path of two story brick homes.

Before we'd gotten a few houses away from the victims in question, I'd parked the truck in a wooded area. There was a path that led from the woods directly behind the soon to be victim's home. Once there, I waved Eve to post up along side the patio door out of sight. It was three o'clock in the morning and all of the lights appeared to be out.

I took the glasscutter out of my back pocket and traced a nice sized circle in the glass slightly above the lock. Once the glass was cut, I took the glass magnet and pulled the glass out of the door, tossing it on the grass. As the rain continued to pour behind me, I reached in and turned the look. I opened the door and stuck my head inside of the house. It smelled like cinnamon.

The heat appeared to be on blast and to my right was a roaring fireplace. The logs that were inside of it crackled like pop rocks. I took the .40 Glock off of my waist and pointed it ahead of me, waving Eve to follow behind. She slipped through the crack of the door and made her way beside me.

"They should be upstairs. Come on," she whispered. I nodded. The carpet felt soft under my Timbs. The house appeared to be nice and cozy. There was a nice, four-piece furniture set in the room we stepped inside of right off the patio. Pictures of the family decorated the big glass table that was in the middle of the room.

I saw there was a father I assumed was our main target, a woman I assumed was his wife, and two little boys that looked to be about the ages of fourteen and fifteen. I continued to creep downstairs until I got to the bottom of the staircase that led us upward.

Eve adjusted her mask and placed her gloved hand on the railing, before making her way upward. I followed closely behind with my ears and eyes on high alert. I figured that since they were supposedly in the witness protection program that we'd run the risk of somebody stopping by to check on them from time to time.

I didn't know if some sort of law enforcement officers patrolled their area, or even went as far as ringing their doorbell to make sure that they were okay. They were on the run from the Cali Cartel and I knew the Cartel to be vicious.

When I reached the top of the stairs, I could hear the sounds of a humidifier somewhere close by. There was a long, carpeted hallway that had four doors in it. All of them were closed with the exception of one. It was the only one opened that had a light shining into the dark hallway. I slowly made my way down the hall with my gun held in front of me with Eve close behind.

I can't lie and say I wasn't paranoid because I was. On top of that, my eyelids were threatening to close because I was so fucking high. I felt giddy and tired at the same time. I came up on the first door in the hallway and began to twist the knob just as the thunder roared in the sky. I could hear the sounds of the rain picking up its intensity. I twisted the knob and slowly pushed the door inward.

When it opened up enough for me to stick my head in, I did. I saw someone lying on the bed with the covers over their head. Whoever it was, was snoring loudly. I crept closer to the bed with the gun in front of me. As soon as I was about a foot away from the sleeping form, suddenly the person threw the covers off of their head, opening their eyes wide.

It looked like the oldest son from the picture. He had blonde hair that was all over his head and a sleep mask pulled across his forehead. He looked as if he was about to scream because he opened his mouth wide. Before any sound came out, I grabbed him by the throat with my left hand and smacked him across the face with my pistol in my right hand. Not once, but twice as hard as I could.

He fell backwards against the sheets with my hand still around his neck. Eve straddled him and pulled the covers all the way back. Underneath, he wore nothing but boxers and ankle socks. She pulled one of her knives from its holster, raised it over her head, bringing it down into his chest so hard, the blade sank into his flesh, leaving only the handle that stuck out of him. Blood squirted up and splashed the sheets.

She pulled the knife all the way out and stabbed him over and over again as if on a rampage. The whole time, I held the boy's neck choking the life out of him, preventing him from making any noise. Although his feet kicked wildly for a second, which caused the bed springs to squeak, that was as bad as it got.

Eve stood up and looked down on her handy work. The boy's body had ten big holes in its torso. Blood oozed out of them like red Kool-Aid and leaked on to the white sheets. She nodded and pulled the blanket back over him. It immediately filled with his blood and became saturated.

We came out of that room and she opened the door to the bedroom directly across from that one. There was a license plate on the door that read, "Privacy". She twisted the knob and stuck her head in as I had done the room before that one. Once she slipped in there, I followed in behind her after looking both ways down the hallway. This is where the sounds of the humidifier came from. It was in the corner of the bedroom right next to a drum set.

On the bed was a tall, blonde-haired teen sleeping on his side. He was shirtless with red swimming trunks on. His eyelids were closed tightly as if he were frowning in his sleep or something. Eve still had blood dripping from her knife. She knelt in front of the sleeping teen and rose the big knife over her head. In one plunge, she brought it down into the side of his neck and mashed the blade inside of it as hard as she could. I could see her arms shaking.

She pulled the knife out and stood up, looking down on her prey. There was a loud gurgling sound along with the sound of the humidifier. I surmised the teen was choking on his own blood. His eyes popped open, but he never made a move to sit up. Blood gushed out of the wound she'd created. He placed his fingers to his throat, trying to swallow then closed his eyes.

He farted loudly before Eve went crazy. She spent the next two minutes stabbing him all over the face and neck. Her blade went in and out of him, splattering blood all over the bedroom. I had to jump back a few times. When she finally finished, the boy's body was half on the bed and half off of it. A pool of his blood decorated the bed and floor. We were on our way out of that room when the lights in the hall way popped on.

"Jacob? Jacob, baby, are you all right in there?" came a female's voice. I could see the light from the hallway under his bedroom door. She pounded on the door again. "Jacob, either you answer me or I'm coming in," she promised.

Eve lowered her eyes and made her way toward the door with the knife in her hand. I could tell she was ready to attack. I waved her off, placing my gun into the small of my back. I then took the serrated deer hunting knife that she'd given me out of its holster and tightened my hand around the handle.

I held it upside down with the blade pointed towards the floor and took a step back. The knob on the door twisted and then very slowly, it came inward. I could smell the scent of a fruity perfume.

"Jacob baby, are you okay in here?" the woman asked, sticking her head through the door. I waited until she stepped into the room before I grabbed her by the throat, slamming led the blade as hard as I could into her chest and pulling it downwards, slicing her wide open. Her blood spilled out of her and over my gloved fist.

I turned her ass around and stepped behind her back, before slicing her from one ear to the next fatality mode. She dropped to the carpet leaking plasma. I took a step back and looked down at my handy work. I was so high, felt absolutely nothing. It seemed like I was in some sort of video game or something.

Eve stepped over her and stuck her head out of the door. She looked to her left then her right, stepping out of the room cautiously. We traveled down the hallway until we got to the end of it. I then moved her out of the way. I stood in front of the last door, grabbed the handle and twisted it. The door swung inward, revealing a man with a shotgun in his hand. I froze in place and waved.

"You son of a bitch. Put your hands up or I swear to God I'll shoot," the man ordered. "You think you can rob me?" his asked as his voice quivered. Half of me was still in the hallway. I slid my gun into the air.

"Look, man. Don't shoot. All I wanted was a television, maybe some jewelry. I'm not even armed," I lied, stepping further into the room with my hands held at shoulders length. He cocked the shotgun and raised it higher on his shoulder.

"Don't you come one step closer. Get on your fucking knees! Now! And where is my wife?" he hollered.

I didn't give a fuck if he had a shotgun or not. I wasn't getting on my knees for no man. His punk ass was going to have to kill me is what I was thinking. I could tell by his body language and the way he held the shotgun, he wasn't a killer. Had I known that he hadn't cocked the shotgun when I'd first stuck my head through the door, I would've ran, bussing his ass before he had the chance. Even though Veeto had said that he wanted the murders done with the knives, I shook my head.

"Look, I got fucked up knees. I can't bend down or else I'd kneel for you," I lied. "I don't want any trouble. Your wife is in Jacob's room. They're both sitting on the bed. My partner has them at gunpoint. If you pull that trigger, he's going to kill both of them. That's a promise. You need to let me go and we'll leave your home empty handed." He shook his head wildly.

"I can't do. I'm sorry, but I'm going to have to turn you and your partner in. I'm calling the authorities." He kept his gun pinned on me and made his way over to the dresser where he grabbed his phone. I took a step forward.

"Look, that is not smart. You do that and your family is dead. Now, you need to let me go. Now!" He raised the shotgun and dropped the phone on the floor. "I'm warning you. I am the best damn deer hunter that New York has ever seen. If you move another inch, I'm gong to blow your fucking head off of your shoulders. Now, lay on the bed. Do it right this instant or else." He stepped closer with the handle of the shotgun pressed up against his shoulder.

"A'ight! A'ight! A'ight!" I held up my hands and made my way to the bed. "You fucking got me. Are you happy? Just tie my wrists and make your fucking call to the police. I'd rather be in their custody then that of a crazed lunatic."

I laid on the bed and placed my arms behind my back, praying that he took the bait. My heart pounded in my chest. I knew we out of there. It felt like we had been in their here to get for more than thirty minutes. I felt like something seriously wrong was about to happen. He slowly made his way in my direction with his shotgun still aimed at me. He stopped at the dresser, opened the top drawer and pulled out a tie, placing it in his mouth. He placed his knee on the bed and grabbed my wrist.

"Just be still and there won't be any further problems." He held the shotgun with one hand, grabbed my wrist and wrapped the silk tie around it, then grabbed the other. The bedroom door swung opened with so much force, it slammed into the wall. He looked up with his eyes wide, aiming his shotgun at the intruder. I knocked it upward.

A round fired into the ceiling, knocking a hole in it. Plaster fell on us in a white smoky cloud. He got ready to cock the shotgun again, when I pulled my gun from the small of my back and slammed the handle directly into the center of his forehead, bustin' it wide open. He fell backward on the bed and rolled to the carpet.

"Oh fuck. Don't do this," he groaned.

Eve ran over with her knife in hand while I straddled him, beating him over the head again and again as I slammed the steel into his soft flesh. Eve knelt down and began to stab him all over the place while I continued to do my thing. I kept on imagining what would have happened had he gotten a round off in me or her.

The vision in my head got me more and more heated. We must have worked on him for a full five minutes. By the time we finished, he was a bloody mess and so were we. But, nevertheless, we'd accomplished the mission and became eighty thousand dollars richer.

Chapter 11

I spent the next few years getting money with my niggas out in Harlem. Every now and then, I'd link up with Eve and we'd hit a major lick for her uncle Veeto. He'd upped our pay and for each murder victim, we received twenty five thousand dollars a piece. For most the most part, the money was good money, but I was eating so good, I'd turned him down more than a few times.

Through my guy Wetto, I was able to lock down ninety nine percent of the Blood niggas out in Spanish Harlem and three decks of Latin Kings that were eating with us. Every time Wetto and I linked up, he wasn't copping no less than a hundred kilos of Vega's heroin at fifty thousand a piece.

Whenever I needed to place an order, I went through my uncle 'cuz I refused to fuck with my father. I still felt like he favored my brother over me, so I didn't need him. I took that shit to heart and rather than taking handouts from him, I did my own thing. Besides, a nigga was eatin' like a fat bitch who got hyped when money was deposited on her link card every month.

Everywhere I went in Spanish Harlem, I was treated like a God. When the Spanish and Black bitches saw me, they rushed me like I was Justin Bieber was in his hay day, pulling on my clothes and trying their damnedest to shove their numbers in my pocket. Didn't matter if they were with their nigga or not, bitches were tryna get in where they fit in. I loved that shit.

While starin' they nigga down, I'd rubbed all over their asses, kiss their necks, allowing them to hug all over me. My disrespectful ass enjoyed making their nigga feel like shit. Wasn't my fault the bitches was choosin'. Them niggas never uttered a word though. I'm guessin' they knew that I was feeding the whole hood and had they crossed any lines, they ran the risk of being thrown over the George Washington Bridge. I took advantage of the power I had.

Tori had managed to hold her in-house position for nearly four years without getting under my skin to the point I was ready to kick her ass out. She was really laid back and stayed to herself, allowing me to spoil her ass.

Ebony became so disgusted by our relationship, she'd given up her custody rights of Maine, handing them to me. I didn't know what kind of a father I was going to, but I tried my best to not think about it.

Tori and Maine had a real close relationship. She acted as if her was her biological son and I was cool with that. I think that's another reason why I'd kept her around so long. Well that and the fact that a nigga caught some serious feelings for her. Her heart was pure.

She understood being with me would cost her her family. She endured the ridicule that came with our relationship like a true champ, then at the same time, stood by my side even though I was a pure street nigga to the core. So, I guess you can say that her, Maine, and I had a little family thing going on behind closed doors. I loved the both of them a lot and all I wanted to do was right by them.

Once Tori received her business management and finance degrees, I allowed her to oversee three beauty salons. Two of them were located in Spanish Harlem and the other was on the black side of Harlem. I'd chosen these spaces because they were Blood territory and after putting out the word of who each spot belonged to, I knew she'd be safe and sound to operate without any problems. My Blood niggas were everywhere and about that life. Especially when it came to Showbiz Vega.

* * *

It was two weeks away from my son's sixth when my whole life began to change for the worst. I'll never forget it. It was mid June and the summer in New York, the sun was scorching. This day, it was a hundred and fifteen degrees outside and humid as fuck. It was so bad, as soon as I stepped out of my Lexus truck to walk up to Eve's stoop, I started to gasping to breathe.

My forehead was peppered with sweat and I felt like my skin was being baked. I jogged up her steps, entered her building and beat on her door. The hallway felt like I was in an oven. I started to beat on it again, not even bothering to wait for her to make it to the door.

"Hold up, hold up. Damn! And stop beating on my muthafucking door!" she yelled in Spanish. There was a brief imagine I could make out. It was the slopes of her supple golden breasts and her belly button with the pink two-carat diamond ring I'd given her about a month prior. Her hair was all over her head. There were bags under her eyes and she smelled a little foul. She wiped her nose with her hand. "Why the fuck you beating on my door like you the police, Juanito?"

She didn't even look up at me. I noted the paint on her toenails needed to be redone. I brushed past her and stepped into her house. It was air conditioned and cool. I breathed in a sigh of relief. That was until I looked around and saw how dirty her place was. There were pizza boxes stacked up on her dining room able and roaches crawling all over them.

There was trash on the floor in a big pile. Clothes were all over the living room, even some thrown over the arms of the couches. It smelled funky. There were a bunch of dishes in the sink. Roaches crawled all over them, as well.

"What the fuck is going on in here? Why is this muhfucka so nasty?" I snapped and mugged her ass. I wasn't with that and Eve and I were a lot alike. I was used to her place being very neat, clean and smelling good.

As far as she went, she was always dressed in the top of the line clothing. Smelled real fine, and looked even better. She was as vain as I was about her appearance and her crib. Seeing that this day blew my mind. She closed the door.

"It's good. I just don't feel like doing shit right now. Damn. Don't come over here getting on my nerves either." She scratched her scalp, then ran her fingers through her hair, before tossing it over her shoulder.

I watched her sit on the couch, go under it, and pull out a Ziploc bag full of aluminum foiled Vega heroin. She pulled out one of the packages and sat it on the table. She then pulled a Crown Royal purple bag from underneath the couch, sitting it beside the dope.

"I lost my father a week ago, Juanito. Somebody robbed his store and caught him off guard. He had a heart attack and died on the spot." She pulled a bunch of work out of the Crown Royal bag, setting them up. She got up, went into the kitchen and came back with a spoon. She plopped down on the couch and poured some of the Vega heroin into it, added water, then flamed the bottom of the spoon.

I sat there dumbfounded because I just knew she wasn't about to do what I think she was. I knew how important he was to her, so I could only imagine what she was going through. Even though he and I had never developed a strong relationship, I respected him because he was her dad. But his death didn't make me feel no type of way. I was only concerned about Eve.

"Yo, I'm sorry to here that, kid. Why you ain't get at me right away after it happened? You know I would have been there for you. We go through everything together. Always." She shook her head.

"I was so fucked up that I didn't want to be bothered. Plus, I figured you'd be all up Tori's ass anyway." She took her needle and drew the dope up into the syringe before setting the spoon on the table. She wrapped a belt around her arm, holding her forearm out, revealing the old needle track marks.

"Yo, so this is what you finna do? You gon' turn into a junkie because your old man died? What type of shit is that, Evelina?" I snapped at her in Spanish.

She poked the needle into her vein and pushed down the feeder. I could tell the poison entered into her system because her eyes rolled into the back of her head and she moaned out loud.

She pulled the syringe out of her and placed it on the table. Her eyes were low. She squeezed her nose and ran her tongue across her lips. "My father was all I really had left, Showbiz. You don't know what it feels like to be all alone, how it feels to hurt every second of every day. I been suffering from depression, dealing with this bipolar bullshit ever since I was a little girl.

Whenever I fell to my lowest point, my father was the only one that could bring me back to reality. Every morning I woke up since the age of twelve, I've wanted to kill myself. I don't know why. Maybe it has something to do with all of the shit that Charlie did to me it's because I was born to hate myself. But either way, I can't take this shit no more, Juanito. I need to escape. Life has become too much for me." She sat back and closed her eyes. Her robe fell open and exposed her breasts.

I stood there speechless after hearing her finally open up. I couldn't believe it. All these years of knowing her, I had overlooked the signs. I always assumed she was stronger than me, that she could handle anything life had thrown at her. I wished she'd come to me sooner. Had I lost her, I would have gone nuts. Eve was a major part of my life, second to my mother. She even came before my own child, my son.

"Eve, I wish you would have come to me. That breaks my heart to hear you've been struggling on your own. I'm supposed to have your back. You was supposed to let me do my job. I love the fuck outta you, girl. You know that shit." She laid her head on the back of the couch and looked up at the ceiling.

"Yeah, well I found my outlet. Ever since I been fucking with this shit from Havana, I been able to go and feel free away from all pain. I was wasting my time with that shit up my nose. This is the life. I feel every effect of the drug that I was supposed to. Everything is heightened by one hundred percent."

She closed her eyes and spread her thighs further apart. I could see right up her robe. She was without panties. It looked like she hadn't shaved her pussy in a few weeks. I lowered my head and took a deep breath.

"So what is your game plan? I mean, is this is it?"

She opened her eyes and leaned forward. She sniffed and pulled on her nose. "I don't have a game plan, Juanito. I don't know what I wanna do with my life. All I wanna do is get high. If ever my money get low, I'll kill a muthafucka and pay me twenty five gees a whop. Long as I got that outlet and a plug on this dope, that's all I need. Besides, it's not like you really give a fuck. You got a whole ass kid to worry about. I'll be okay."

She struggled when she finally made it to her feet. She staggered to stand up a little bit before getting her balance. She scratched her head before she got up to get something to drink. "I'm thirsty."

She walked on her bare feet. With every step she took, the roaches all over the floor scattered in a million different directions. She continued to walk across the floor as if nothing was happening down below.

I covered my face with both of my hands. I didn't now what to say, do, or think. I was confused. All I knew was that I loved her. She was my right hand. It broke my heart to see her in such a state. She opened the refrigerator.

"Damn, it ain't nothing to eat in this muhfucka and it stank." She slammed the door so hard, the box of Captain Crunch that was on top of it f the floor. She stepped on the box and came back into the living room and sat on the couch. "I'm so fucking high right now." I uncovered my face and looked across the table a her.

"Eve, I don't like seeing you like this. This shit's killing me." I swallowed and felt my stomach turn. She wiped her mouth with the back of her hand.

"I don't know what to tell you, Juanito. This is me. Shit don't always work out in the way you plan it for it to. I used to think I'd grow up and be a model or a movie star, but I ain't gon' be shit but a drug addict. It is what it is. I'm gon' go out that is. At least I'ma die happy."

She grabbed the spoon and poured about a gram into it, before following the same process that she'd followed before. After she finished, she drew the dope into the syringe and smacked her inner forearm. I felt like I couldn't breathe. It was like watching your mother or somebody you cared about dying in front of you. All I wanted to do was take away her pain. I wanted her to fee better.

"Eve, what can I do to make you feel better? How can I take you away from the pain that you're feeling?" She pumped more of the dope into her system and laid her head back, biting on her bottom lip. Both of her nipples were out of her robe and stood erect. She crossed her thighs and squeezed them together.

"You can't do nothing but support me, Juanito. This is who I am now. You gotta love me through this shit. As long as I've been apart of your life, I have never judged you. I've always gon' with the flow. That's what love is when it's unconditional anyway." She rubbed her nose.

I sat there looking at her from across the table with a million thoughts running through my head. She and I had been nearly the same person every since we were in the ninth grade. Eve had become all I've ever known. She was my chick. My right hand. My heart and soul. The only person I fully trusted in this world. There was nothing that I wouldn't do for her or to a muthafucka about her. She was my everything. So when I looked across that table and saw what she'd become in such a small amount of time, I felt my heart breaking in two.

"Well, Evelina. I love you, boo. I swear to God, I do. I'll do anything for you. And I'll accept you for who you are. But this here is literally too much for me to witness. I gotta go because if I stay, I'ma do something that I don't want to do. I can't take this shit."

I stood up preparing to leave her place. I felt dizzy and my heart was pounding in my cheat. I was having a hard time catching my breath. She slid her hand into the couch, and pulled out .45 handgun. She cocked it and slammed it on the table.

"You wanna help me, Juanito, then kill me!" she screamed. "'Cause I can't take this shit no more!" Tears sailed down her cheeks. I stood there for a long time without saying a single word to her. I exhaled and ran my left hand over my stomach. Once again, it felt like it was somersaulting inside of me.

"Eve, you're real high and you're bugging right now. You don't mean that shit." I looked down into her eyes as he tears slid down my cheeks.

"I wish we would have never killed Charlie. I didn't want to kill my brother, but you made us. Now that my father is gone, he's going to run into Charlie up there and he's going to tell him what I did. My dad will never love me anymore. I don't have anybody." She broke into a fit of tears shaking her head from side to side. Then her face turned into a snarl. She grabbed the gun and slammed it on the table. "Kill me, Juanito! Kill me. I swear to God you better kill me or you're going to regret it. We should have never done that to Charlie. What the fuck was I thinking?" She hollered so loud, I was sure the neighbors heard her.

I lowered my head and sighed. "Eve, you need to calm yo' ass down. Everything is going to be all right. You're just going through something right now. Put the gun on the table and let me hold you for a minute. We can get through this shit together. I ain't about to kill you. I love you too much."

Tears were flowing freely from my eyes. I felt like I was on the verge of losing my mind all together. I was trying to summon the orders that would make her feel all better. I needed her beside me. She picked up the gun and pointed it at her head.

"I swear to God that if you don't do it, I will. I don't want you to fucking hold me like I'm some helpless bitch. I want you to put one in my dome and send me on my way. I don't want to be here any more. I'm tired."

She cocked the hammer. I sat on the couch across from her, looking into her eyes the whole time. "So you finna go out like a punk bitch, right? All this time I was thinking you was a killer and shit, it turns out that you ain't nothing but a fucking coward. You make me sick. I don't know this person that's in front of me right now. So, if you wanna pull that trigger, then gon' head, Pussy. What's stopping you?" I spat with such venom.

I was praying my words to her would do the opposite of killing herself. I was hoping that they'd allow her to see that she wasn't as weak as she thought she was, that there was nothing soft about her. I mean I didn't know what else to do. I was at a loss for words.

I'd never been in any position like that one. I was used to Eve being hard and savage-like. I didn't think she needed me to try and sweet talk her like I would another female. She frowned and more tears ran out of her eyes.

'That's how you feel, Showbiz? That's what's inside of your heart?" She took the gun away from her temple and placed it inside of her mouth before pulling the trigger.

Boom!

I watched her brains blow out the back of her head. She fell forward and her face bounced off of the table. Blood gushed out of the hole in her head. I could smell the scent of her flesh in the air. I sat on the couch stunned. My heart felt as if it was in my mouth. My eyes were big as paper plates.

My entire world was spinning so fast, I couldn't think. Over and over again, the image of her brains being blown out the back of her head played before my eyes until I snapped out of it, rushing to her side. I held her and I cried like a big ass baby.

"Evelina! Evelina! Why did you do that shit, Evelina? Oh my God, ma! Don't you know how much I need you?" I cried, rocking her back and forth.

Her eyes remained wide open. I could feel her blood all over my arms. It was hot and slick like a thick version of motor oil. All of the images of our childhood played before my mind. I couldn't believe that she done what she'd did. I cried and cried, before placing my hand on her.

I couldn't believe that she was gon', feeling nothing in her chest. Nothing in this world could have prepared me for what she'd done. I kissed her all over her face. I wished that I had said more kind words, that I had treated her better.

"Eve, please don't die on me, Ma. I need you." I rocked with her for two hours straight. When I finally got up, I was drenched in her blood. I was somewhat at peace with what had taken place, although I knew I'd never recover from it.

Chapter 12

I fell off the wagon after Evelina's death. About a week later, I found myself locked in my basement with a kilo of heroin in front of me, tooting gram after gram. Even though the heroin was rich, just a little bit got me so high that I couldn't feel my face or hands. I kept right on tooting, getting higher and higher. To be honest, I think I was trying to kill myself without actually admitting it. Everyday I woke up without Eve by my side, was a day that I felt an emotional pain I couldn't bare it.

You see, prior to her death, I never had a reason to be emotional. My heart was cold and always had been. I never dwelled on shit. If something tragic happened, I dealt with it and kept it moving, but her death was a game changer for me. I never knew how much I really cared about her until she was gone.

Now that she was, I couldn't fathom moving forward without her. I made a thick line of Vega heroin, leaned forward and tooted it hard. So hard, I wound up coughing. I had to beat my fist on my chest. My eyes were low and there were loud bells in my ears. I kept seeing her face and every time, I prepared another line.

There was a knock at the basement door. The sudden noise caught me off guard, causing me to perk up. "Damn! Who the fuck is it?" I hollered.

"Baby, it's your brother, Tristian. He's on the phone. He says he needs to talk to you. Are you gonna take it?" Tori asked through the door.

I jumped off of the couch and put my hand through the door until she placed the phone in my hand. As soon as it was there, I slammed the door back and walked sat on the couch.

"What's up, Tristian? Now ain't a good time." I leaned down and tooted another line. My heart was racing so fast, my head was spinning. My whole body began to itch like crazy. I could feel the veins throbbing all over me.

"What it do, big bruh? Yo, I'm just calling to make sure you're straight. I heard about what happened to Eve and I ain't heard from you in a minute." I sat my back on the couch and placed my hand over my heart that was thumping in my chest. I took a deep breath to calm myself.

"Yo, I'm good as can be, kid. Just taking a load off. You know how it is. What's good wit' you?" I bugged my eyes out of my head and struggled to breathe. I felt like I was being twisted into a knot.

"Fucking around in Cancun. Just got here yesterday. I'm trying to see what these Mexicans hoez on down here. Nah'mean? I can't get you off my brain, though." I got on my knees and placed my hand over my hear. I winced in pain. I couldn't breathe.

"Yo, like I said. I'm good. Nah'mean? I wanna fuck wit' you when you get back in town, though. Think we need to sit down as brothers and get an understanding." I struggled to stand up, using the arm of the couch. I got to my feet and placed my back against the wall, slowly sliding down it until my knees were at my chest.

"That sound like a plan, Dunn. Yo, you already know Pops trying to fuck wit' you. He feel real bad about how you been snubbing him and shit. You already know he one of them emotional types. No matter what y'all got going on, you're still his first born. He talk about you all the time. He said he just wants y'all to get an understanding. How do you feel about that?"

My chest felt as if it were being ripped open. Reluctantly, tears slid down my cheeks. I gritted my teeth and laid on my back. "That's cool, Tristian. I'll hit his phone in a day or so. I'ma get at you, though. Hold ya head up, kid."

I got ready to drop the phone beside me. I was struggling to breathe. "Bruh, when you get a chance, check on Kalani for me. She staying at my crib until I get back in New York. Just make sure that everything is everything. Nah'mean?"

"I got you." I ended the call and dropped the cell beside me. I grabbed a hunk of my chest and squeezed it. I couldn't understand what was going on with me. I was thinking that I might have been way too high. My entire face was sweaty. I couldn't feel my fingers when I balled them into fists. And my throat was so dry, I couldn't swallow no matter how hard I tried. I was starting to panic. I sat up on one elbow. "Tori!" I yelled and scooted backwards until my back was the wall.

I waited to hear her footsteps or the sound of some but none came. Blood dripped out of my nose onto my opened my mouth as I tried to breathe, feeling a bunch of bubbles traveling up my throat. I tried to call out to her again, but I couldn't. I was too weak. My throat too dry. I closed my eye as they rolled into the back of my head and passed out.

* * *

I stood in front of the bright sun, its rays warming my skin. I had to raise my hand to shield my eyes because it was so bright. I looked to my left and right and saw I was somewhere on a beach. The waves of the water crashed into each other, then onto the shore where I stood frozen, unable to move. As I continued to shield my eyes, I looked out into the big body of water, and saw a figure walking on top of it. From the distance, I couldn't make out any facial features, but there was no doubt in my mind that this figure was, Evelina.

Her long curly hair flowed behind her. She wore a white gown that clung to her body. The material so sheer, I could tell she was naked underneath. She walked toward me and the closer she got, the dimmer the sun became until it set behind the water. Only then was I able to make out that it was Evelina completely.

She walked another fifty yards and then onto the white sand. Once here, she continued toward me with her eyes looking into that of my own. Now twenty feet away and the spell I had been under was broken. I was able to move my legs. I took off running in her direction.

I couldn't believe that she was alive. Knew I'd had to have imagined the entire suicide. She was too strong to submit to weakness. We were too much alike. We'd rather be shot by the bullets of someone else's gun then that of our own.

She lowered her head and took off running in my direction. As soon as she got within five feet, she jumped and I braced myself to catch her. She landed in my arms, wrapping hers around my neck.

"Juanito, you came. You finally came to save me. I knew you'd come." She kissed my lips. Sucked all over them. I could hear the deep moans coming from her throat, causing my manhood to rise. After kissing her lips, I set her down on her bare feet, looking down on her.

"I thought you left me, Eve. I thought that you left me behind in that cold ass world, ma." She looked into my eyes and smiled.

"But you came, Juanito. You've actually come to rescue me. I love you so much." Her voice began to crack. It became distorted. "I love you, Juanito." The hold around my neck grew tighter and tighter. She started to choke me. "Juanito! Juanito! Help me! Help! Me!" She took one of her arms from around my neck, reached into the sky and stabbed a big needle into my chest.

"Wake up, Juanito." Her voice grew deeper and deeper. "Wake up, Juanito!" She pushed the needle further into my chest.

The sun reappeared, blinding me. I tried to shield my eyes and take her arm from around my neck, but it was no use. I was frozen again, unable to move. I closed my eyes, preparing to die.

***

Sweat poured down my face. I woke up to the sounds of constant beeping. I opened my eyes and looked up into the face of my old man. He had a snarl on his face that told me he was extremely upset. I tried to sit up in the hospital bed, then felt my I.V. almost dislodged from my veins.

There was an oxygen mask on my face and the sheets that were on top of my body felt like they were suffocating me. I kicked my legs wildly, trying to get them off of me. My father placed his forearm into my chest.

"Calm own, mijo. Calm down," he said in Spanish. "You're okay. I got you now."

Tori rushed to my bedside with tears running down her cheeks. "Oh, Showbiz. I thought you died, baby. I swear to God I thought you died. I don't know what I would have done if you had."

She grabbed my hand and kissed the back of it. I opened my eyes wide and looked her over. My father took a step back and shook his head. I could feel my heart pounding in my chest. I swallowed and took the oxygen mask off my face.

"What happened to me? Why am I laying in this hospital bed?" I asked, swallowing my spit.

"Baby, you overdosed. I found you in the basement laid up against the wall with foam coming out of your mouth. Luckily, I had some Narcan in my purse. I had from when our uncle overdosed. My aunt had used it on him and saved his life. She said that every person who had a spouse that used heroin needs to keep some of that stuff on them. Thankfully, I took her advice. After I administered it to you, your father just so happened to be pulling up to our home. He brought you over her and you've been here for two days. Thank God that you're all right."

"And Evelina? Where is she? Is she down the hall?" I asked, looking from Tori to my father. My father frowned.

"She's dead, Juanito, and you need to get over it or you're going to join her. I did not raise you to become a fucking addict. You're supposed to be a better man than this. How will I leave you everything that I've built if you insist on putting that poison up your nose? The doctors said you had over five ounces of heroin in your system. Do you realize that you can be dead right now?" he snapped in Spanish.

My father was about 5'10" with golden-colored skin and light brown eyes he'd passed down to all of his children. He had wavy black hair with specks of gray in it. He was dressed in a tailored Italian Armani suit with a red and black tie to match his leather shoes.

"Pop, I love that girl, man. Eve was my heart and soul. I just got to tooting and I wasn't even thinking about the amount I was consuming. I just needed the pain to go away. Fuck man, I miss her. I saw her in my dream." I squeezed my eyelids tightly, wishing that it was her face I had awakened to.

"Well, it was stupid. She's gone. Crying won't bring her back, so get yourself together because this is a horrendous sight!" he spat.

I nodded. "A'ight. I just need a lil' time. I'll be good in a few days.

"You don't have a few days. You'll be discharged this afternoon. I'll give you the rest of the night to get yourself together, then you and I have to have a serious talk. It's time for you to live up to your responsibilities as the oldest Vega child. I mean it, mijo. You've played around in those streets long enough. It's time for you to learn the ways of the Vegas. You understand me?" He frowned before he walked out of the room. "I'll see you first thing in the morning. Later."

He opened the door and I saw the two big Cuban bodyguards that often followed him around as security. They waited for him to lead the way before they trailed him. I laid my head back on the pillow and sighed.

***

Tori picked up the pillow in my master bedroom and fluffed it before setting it back on the bed. "Here you go, baby. Just lay back and let me take care of you. Okay?" She guided me backward on the bed.

As soon as my head hit the pillow, I felt like I was about to throw up. "Yo, watch out, ma."

I jumped up and took off running for the bathroom. Once there, I fell to my knees and gagged over the toilet. My stomach felt like it was being ripped out of my torso. I spit and prayed that something would come up to help relieve the pain I felt deep within my gut. My face was drenched in sweat. My mouth was so dry, it tasted like sand. I felt as if I were going to pass out. "Tori! Come here, baby! Hurry up." I called to her.

"What's the matter, baby?" she rubbed my back. "Damn, boo. You are burning up. Should I call the ambulance?"

Maine walked into the bathroom door with his tablet in hand. "Tori, what's wrong with my dad? Is he goin' to be okay?" Worry was plastered over his face.

"Maine, I'm good. Go to your room. I need to talk to Tori right now."

I looked up at Tori. "Baby, you go into the bottom drawer of my dresser and get my dope for me. I'm sick and it's the only thing that'll help me through."

She shook her head. " I'm not getting' you no more fuckin' heroin, Showbiz. Boy, you damn near died. Don't you get that?" she knelt beside me, rubbing my back some more.

I placed my face deep within the porcelain bowl and regurgitated the remaining contents of my breakfast. I could no longer contain my bowels either. "Tori, I swear fo' God, if I gotta get up and get my shit myself, I'ma fuck you up. Bitch, go get my shit! I'm sick. I just need a quick fix." I tried my best to gather my bearings and stand, but I grew weaker by the minute.

"No! I refuse to participate in that. I love you too fucking much, Showbiz." She backed out of the bathroom

I continued to purge my guts. I felt so weak and dazed. "You don't love me, bitch! If you loved me, you'd do what the fuck I say. I'm kicking yo' ass out. I swear I am. I'ma find me a bitch that do what the fuck I say."

I fell to my stomach and began to drag myself across the floor toward my bedroom, my elbows digging into the floor boards until they met my bedroom carpet. Regardless of how shitty I felt, I kept crawling.

Tori slid down to the floor landing on her butt. She cried as she watched me make my way toward my dresser.

"Please stop, Showbiz. You don't need it. You're better than that," she whimpered.

"Shut up, bitch. You don't give a fuck about me." I crawled even more. "Can't believe this how you get down. I hate you right now."

Even though I'd said that, I didn't really mean it. I knew she felt was doing the right thing. She had to, knowing how much pain and suffering I was experiencing by not having the drug in my system. I felt like I was literally being torn apart. Withdrawing off heroin was the worst feeling in the world.

"Don't say that shit, Showbiz. I love you to death. Please, don't say that to me." She cried into her hands and covered her face. Her knees were on the back of her hands. She looked like a human ball.

I got to the dresser and pulled the drawer open, tossing the pajamas out and over my shoulder. I rummaged around until I came upon the kilo of Vega heroin. I pulled it out and set it on the carpet. As soon as I saw the aluminum packaging with the Cuban flag on it, my body began to shake from anticipation.

"Don't do this, Showbiz. I am begging you," Tori cried.

Maine came and stood in the doorway. "Tori, why are you crying?"

I ripped open the packaging and exposed the contents. I placed my nose right on the brick and snorted with my right nostril as hard as I could. The dope rushed up my nose and directly to my brain. I started to feel all of the withdrawal symptoms fading away fast. I laid my left nostril on the brick and tooted as hard as I could, before rolling onto my back.

I could feel the drug taking its effect all over my body. I went from feeling sick, dazed and confused, to happy, joyful, and euphoric in a matter of sixty seconds. I ran my tongue across my teeth and smiled. Heroin was my oasis.

Chapter 13

My Pops made it seem like he needed to speak with me urgently the next morning. When I called him, he'd said he was out of town on business and he'd be back later that night. Tristian called me up first thing the next morning and, once again, asked me to go over to check on Kalani. He said he just wanted to make sure that she was okay. I guessed my father hadn't told him about me over dosing because he'd never brought it up and neither did I.

Instead, I jumped out of the bed and took a shower. After getting squeaky clean, I sat on the lid of the toilet and tooted two grams of Vega heroin. The drug rushed into my system and had me feeling like a champion in a matter of seconds.

I got dressed in a black and red Robert Cavalli fit and threw on the matching Balenciagas before opening the door to my bathroom. Tori set on the edge of the bed, tying up her Airmax. She looked up at me and flared her nostrils.

"Good morning, baby. How are you feeling?" she asked dryly.

I kissed her on the forehead. "I'm alive and strong. What more can I possibly ask for?" I pulled her up and into my embrace. "Come here, girl!"

She shrieked and beat her fists on my chest. "Stop, Showbiz. You gon' make me late for work." She tried to wiggle from my grasp.

"Yo, boo. I appreciate what you tried to do yesterday, but this heroin ain't like no weed. Once your body gets a high, you gotta it have it or it'll fuck you up. I got better control of it now. I ain't gon' go crazy no more like I did last week. I was just grieving. That's my word." I tried to kiss her, but she moved her head out of the way.

"Naw, gone because yesterday you had such negative shit to say. Talking about kicking me out and everything. You called me so many bitches. Had me feelin' like shit. Thought we was better than that."

I hugged her tighter, planting kisses all over her face. "You see when I ain't got my medicine, everything goes haywire. I felt like shit. I thought we were better than that. You know I ain't mean none of that shit. You're my boo thang. I'll murk something over you." I smacked her on that fat ass.

"Umm hmm. Yeah, I guess." She kissed my lips and laid her head on me. "Promise me, Showbiz, that you ain't gon' take that much no more. Please. I don't know what I would do without you. You got me living a life style that I'm so addicted to now. I been rocking the latest of everything since I been your woman. You got me boujee as hell."

I laughed and nodded my head. "Rightfully so. You fucking wit' Showbiz, baby. The sky is the muthafucking limit!" I grabbed that ass and tongued her down.

* * *

Two hours later, I copped me a Porsche 911 GT3, all red with the black and red Fazzio rims. It had all white leather seats and a top that dropped into the Porsche's trunk so I could really stunt on niggas. I was planning on putting televisions all throughout that bitch and my name stitched into the headrests. I had a knack for hooking up my whips.

I was one of those that gotta have the best of the best whip type of niggas. I loved stunting on others and making feel less than. I didn't honestly know why I was like this, but I was. It took me another hour before I was able to drive off of the lot with the Porsche. The salesmen who sold the whip took forever wit' the paperwork, but after it was all said and done, I pulled of the lot just as the sun peeked through clouds.

There was no humidity in the city and it looked as if it was set to be a beautiful day. I dropped the hard top and turned up the "Apeshit" track by the Carters as I sped through the streets of New York. I was high and feeling like a boss. I was thankful to be alive, while missing the fuck out of Evelina.

I pulled up to Tristian's brownstone out in Brooklyn and saw Kalani sitting on the stoop in some tight pink Fendi shorts with her laptop on her lap, a cup of Starbucks coffee and some books on each side of her. She had a pair of pink and black Cartier sunglasses on her face. Her hair was pulled back into a neat ponytail.

She looked focused on the computer. I pulled all up on the curb. The block looked packed. Damn near on every stoop I looked on, there were more than a few people sitting on it, looking in my direction. A bunch of them were females that had that look like, "He look like my next baby daddy."

Some of the shorties had put up a basketball hoop in the middle of the street and were balling about ten deep. I saw about six little girls playing hopscotch on the side across the street from Tristian's brownstone.

There was also a group of girls about five deep playing double dutch. There were a few niggas out there too, washing their mediocre ass whips, but I wasn't paying them no mind. I had a .45 and a Tech .9 under the seat ready for whatever a nigga felt like pulling.

I felt the sun shining down hard on my head. "Yo, Kalani. What it do, ma?" I hollered up at her. She pulled her glasses down on her nose and looked out at me before she stood up. Her thick thighs jiggled as she dusted her ass off.

"Showbiz, what are you doing in Brooklyn? I thought you was one of them Harlem niggas," she joked, coming down the stairs toward the Porsche. I waited until she was leaning over the passenger's door before I responded.

"Shorty, you know what it is. I'm Harlem through and through, but I got a call from Tristian. He told me to stop by and check on you, so that's what I'm doing." I sucked my lips. "I see you out here lookin' good as hell while he's vacationing in Cancun. What's all that about?"

I could see her big nipples poking through her halter top. Man, this woman was so fucking fine. I didn't know how my brother had locked her ass down. There was a light breeze that caused her long pony tail to sway with it.

"Am I supposed to be out here looking ugly as hell?" She sucked her teeth. "Never that though. I guarantee Tristan ass ain't down there looking all rough and rugged. That man probably tip top from head to toe with a fresh lining. You know how he get down." She looked down the block at the little girls arguing over who was next to jump.

"Yeah, he probably is, but that ain't my concern. I'm tryna see what's good with you. Why don't you roll through the city with me for a minute? Let's catch up. I can use a lil' female companionship."

She looked up at me and blushed, before lowering her head. "That sounds like a plan. Let me just get my stuff from inside. I'll cruise with you, especially since you rollin' like this. When you gon' talk yo' brother into gettin' one?" She laughed, eyeing the interior of my whip.

I shrugged. "I guess once he get his money right. But you gotta put some work in to be able to cop one of these jokas. You think you got that typa work ethic?" I asked, looking into her pretty eyes.

She shrugged, smiling. Her deep dimples appeared, prominent on both cheeks. She broke eye contact with me and looked back down the street. The little girls were fighting like cats and dogs. "Damn, lemme go grab my stuff before somebody start shooting. I see why you don't come to Brooklyn regularly."

She jogged up the steps and gathered her belongings to take back inside. I couldn't help but notice how her shorts went all up her ass. I felt my dick stir. She disappeared inside, then came back five minutes later. She'd slipped into a pink pleated Fendi skirt and matching top. She wore sandals that showed off her pretty manicured toes. She opened the door and slid into my whip, smelling all good and shit.

"A'ight, I'm ready to roll. And for the record, I do think that I am worth a car like this one day. I'm going to get it. All I have to do is apply myself and when the time is right, it'll happen."

Instead of driving forward, I backed the Porsche off the block because the street ahead of us was packed with about twenty bodies fighting like crazy. Mothers of several neighborhood kids had gotten involved. It looked so chaotic, I wanted sound my gun off so everybody would scatter, but I decided against it and pulled off.

I looked over at Kalani's fine ass. Her caramel skin was glowing. Lips were juicy and painted with lip gloss. She had light freckles covering her face that were barely noticeable. Her thighs were so deliciously thick, I couldn't help but eye them with hunger.

I knew she was my brother's bitch and all, but shorty was bad. Tens across the board and I considered myself a tough critic.

"Yo, I see you went in there and transformed and shit. You ain't have to do that for lil' ol' me." I laughed, stepping on the gas a little. I didn't have a destination in mind. I just wanted to roam around the city with a bad bitch in the passenger seat. You know how that shit go.

She smacked her lips. "I ain't go in there and put this on for you. Them shorts was just ridin' too far up in the wrong places and I thought this attire was a little more appropriate."

"Yeah, a'ight. Let's go wit' that then. Anyway, how you been doin'? How's school comin' along?"

"I'm grindin' you can say. Tryin' to get that young bachelor's of science degree so I can make somethin' of myself. I'm the first one of all my mother's kids to be accepted into and attend college. My goal is to finish with honors and put my degrees to good use. What about you? How've you been? I'm sorry to hear about Eve. I know y'all were extremely close. Wasn't she your woman or somethin' like that?" She looked over at me.

I stormed passed a yellow light and hit a hard left once I got to the intersection, stepping on the gas. At the mention of Eve's name, my stomach started doing somersaults. Immediately I needed my daily fix. I missed Eve like crazy. I swallowed the lump that formed in my throat.

"Yeah, she used to be my lil' lady back when we were in grade school and through the ninth grade. But after that, we just became good friends. I loved her with all my heart and still do. That's my lil' one right there for real. Word up."

Kalani reached over and touched my hand. "I'm sorry. I shouldn't have brought her up. I just wanted you to know I heard and have been praying for you. I know you're strong and I know you'll get through it. But if there's anything I can do for you, please let me know."

I smiled. "I appreciate that, shorty. Just keep hitting me with them dimples while we're together today and I'll emerge stronger than I have any other day she's been gone." I picked her hand up and kissed the back of it.

She blushed, pulling her hand away, then smiled as she made herself comfortable in her seat.

***

We wound up throwing darts at balloons at Coney Island. She'd already popped three of hers and I'd only hit two of mine. We had six darts a piece. I wasn't trying to let her show me up, but my high had come down and I started feeling sick again.

She threw another dart, popping another balloon. "Yeah, Showbiz. You came over here thinkin' you was gon' win *me* a stuffed animal, but Im'a win *you* one. You my son, word is bond! Brooklyn in da house!" She tossed another dart, popping another balloon yet again.

A crowd of people formed behind us awaiting their turn. The air surrounding us smelled of pizza and beer. After tossing a few more darts, I wound up losing. I ain't even gonna lie, I was irritated like a muthafucka. I didn't like losing and the fact that she was a girl made it worse.

"Which teddy bear do you want? Any one you choose is on me," she jacked.

"Man, I don't want none of them shits, ma."

"Aww, Showbiz. It's just a game, Dunn. We just havin' fun. I mean, I am anyway." She pointed to a bear that was dressed as a black panther. "Lemme get that one right there for Maine. I know kid'll like it, won't he?" she asked.

I wrapped my arm around my stomach. "Yeah, he into that shit real tough. Aye look, I'll be back. I gotta use the bathroom real quick." I looked around to locate the nearest restroom or Port a John.

"Wait, hold up. I gotta use the restroom, as well. Come on, I'll go with you." She grabbed her bear from the Carnie, holding it in front of her. It looked as if it were about five feet tall. She was having a hard time carrying since she was only 5'6" or so.

As soon as I got to the bathroom, I rushed into the stall, closed the lid to toilet and pulled my heroin out. I sprinkled some of it on to the back of my hand and tooted it hard. Then poured some more out of the envelope on to the back of my hand and sniffed it up my other nostril. I waited for the effect to kick in, but it wasn't as strong as it had been in the past. I cupped my hand, poured a thicker amount and snorted it all. I poured and snorted until the bells sounded in my ears. My eyes got low and my dick got hard. I knew then I was good to go.

When I got back outside, Kalani was balancing the big bear in her arms. "Yo, let's go ride on the Ferris Wheel or something."

"Boy, these mosquitoes biting like a muthafucka out here. I'm ready to go. Plus, this bear about as big as me." She handed it to me and smiled.

I threw it to the ground and pulled her by the hand. "A'ight, lets bounce and stop and get something to eat."

As I was pulling her along through the crowd, I noticed she kept on looking back at the bear as if she wanted to go back and get it.

"Damn, all that hard work for nothing," she grumbled.

Chapter 14

I sat in front of the big screen television watching *Superfly* with Kalani right beside me. She was on her stomach with a slice of meat lover's pizza in her hand. Her mouth was full of food and she kept on chewing. The way she was positioned, her little skirt rose up on her thick thighs. She smelled so good.

I think the fact that she was my brother's broad was getting to me. Her skin was looking good enough to eat. I could have sworn that I could smell her cat through her skirt. I laid on my side and leaned my face closer to her ass, sniffing the air.

She looked back at me with grease covering her big lips. "What are you doing, Showbiz?"

I laughed. "I ain't doin' nothin' but smellin' your perfume." I took another whiffed and smiled.

She sat up. "Boy, that's weird. I don't know how y'all get down over there in Harlem, but out here in Brooklyn, they consider sniffing another person to be weird and out of pocket. Especially if that person don't belong to you." She rolled her eyes and stood up. Her skirt rose just a tab. She pulled it back over her big booty and popped back on her legs. "What you about to get into 'cuz I'm gettin' a lil' sleepy. I still got some studying to do, as well." She placed her hand on her hip, looking down at me.

I stood up and wiped my hand on the napkin I held in my right hand. "Yo, I got a bottle of Patron and Moet in there. You about to get a lil' toasty wit' me and I ain't takin' no for an answer. Don't worry. I'll help you study the morning. Nah'mean?" I walked into the dining room and grabbed the bottle of Patron, pulling the cork out and turning it up.

She came in the room. "Showbiz, what would yo' brother say if he found out that you were here with me at midnight like you are right now? Wouldn't he snap the fuck out?" she asked.

I shrugged my shoulders. "I don't know and I don't give a fuck. That fool in Cancun living it up. I'm here in Brooklyn making sure you good. Now pop a bottle wit' me. Here." I handed her the bottle of Patron. She took it and took a sip from it, making up her face, and wiping her mouth.

"Damn, that's harsh. I'm a lightweight. I can't be fuckin' with nothin' this heavy." She handed it back to me. "Here, but I'll definitely sip that Moet, though. I know that cost some money." I handed her the bottle.

"Oh, so you got champagne taste, huh?" I walked into the front room and turned on my brother's stereo system. I put on some Meek Mill. I stepped back into the living room and reached for Kalani's hand as Meek Mill's "Whatever You Want" played in the background. "Yo, show me how y'all get down out here in Buck Town. Word up." I grabbed her hand and pulled her to my body.

She crashed into me, spilling a bit of Moet on the carpet, laughing. "Damn, you're aggressive as hell, Showbiz." She took another sip of the Moet and started to groove just a little bit.

"Turn around, ma. I want all of that ass on me." I turned her around and held on to her waist. Her big booty conformed to my lap. I placed my chin on her shoulder and sniffed her up a little more.

A black woman's scent was second to none in my book. I wrapped my forearm around the front of her waist and pulled her back into me. I was hard as hell and needed her to feel it.

"Uh un, Showbiz! Damn, what you on?" she asked, tucking in her bottom lip.

I slid my hands up until I was cupping her perfect titties. I sucked on her neck. "I want some of this pussy, Kalani. This will stay between you and I. You got my word on that." I licked into her ear and sucked on the lobe. "I want this pussy."

She took another swallow of the Moet and sat the glass on the table. She arched her back and planted her ass right on my hard dick. "I'm not gonna do Tristian like that. That's daddy right there. And that nigga would kill you and me. You know he would."

I pulled on her hard nipples and squeezed the mounds of her breasts. I sucked harder on her neck and humped into her ass. "What he don't know won't hurt him I'm on some one night shit. Don't make me take this pussy. I ain't got problem doing that either. Then it'll be all my fault." I bit into her neck hard enough to break the skin.

"Ooohh, stop doing that. Just let me go, Showbiz. Let me walk you to the door because you're drunk right now. I ain't gon' hold none this against you."

I pulled her skirt up her thighs and slid my hand down the front, rubbing her pussy lips through the yellow satin material. She tried to squeeze her thick thighs together, but all she did was trap my big hands between them. I slid it upward and into her panties. Her freshly shaved pussy was as fat as I imagined.

The heat that radiated between her folds damn near seared my hand.

I turned her around and pushed her up against the wall, sucking on her lips with my hand in her panties. "I want some of this pussy, Kalani. You gon' give me some of this shit, one way or the other." I knelt down and tried to suck her pussy through the panties. My tongue ran up and indentation of her sex. I could taste the saltiness on the crotch. It drove me nuts. My dick hopped up and down inside of my pants.

She spread her thighs slightly. "This what you gonna do, Showbiz? You gon' do me like this?" I yanked her panties to the side, exposing her gap. The lips were fully engorged. Her inner lips came slightly past her outer ones. I spread them open with my thumb, revealing her pink hole. I slurped up and down her crease, trapping each lip into my mouth, before suffocating her clitoris.

"Aw, Showbiz. Stop. Please stop me doing like this," she whimpered, grabbing the back of my head. She opened her thighs wider, slowly humping into my face with her eye closed. "Damn, Showbiz. What are you doin' to me?"

I sucked harder on her clit, running my tongue in and out of her tight hole, tasting her juices. I could smell her essence coupled with a hint of sweat. The image of how her thighs looked when we were walking around Coney Island crossed my mind.

I knew at that time that if I had to, I was going to take her pussy. I had to have some of it. Kalani was too bad in my opinion. She opened her thighs wide as wide as they could go, grabbed the sides of my head and rode my face with her big titties, bouncing up and down in her halter. The nipples were poking through fully erect.

"You gone make me do this. You gone take this pussy, daddy. Well take it. Take it. Take it. Take it. Aww, shit! Take it!" She started riding my face so fast and hard, all on my tongue. "Aww. Aww. Aww. Aww, daddy! Daddy! I'm cumming! Aww, fuck," she moaned and came all over my face. Then I stood up and licked her juices and down her wet slit.

I swallowed and wrapped my fist into her hair, pulling her halter over her breasts. "My turn. Now daddy wants you to suck his dick, baby. Come on, Kalani. Show me how y'all get down in Brooklyn. I just gave you some of that Harlem head." I pulled my dick out, stroking him up and down, looking at her hard, beautiful nipples.

She shook her head. "N'all, I don't suck nobody's dick but Tristian's. You ain't my man. I can't do that."

"Bitch, what?" I pulled on her hair, grabbing the base of my dick and put him to her lips. "Open yo' mouth and stop playing wit' me. Get daddy off right now, ma. I thought you was gon' be mine fo' the night."

"Ugh! Okay, but no fucking. I ain't gon' cheat on my man."

She wrapped her lips around my head and sucked it into her mouth like a lollipop. Then she popped it back up at me, before licking all around the head. "This how we do it in Brooklyn, kid." She sucked it back in, pulled it back out of her mouth and drug her lips almost to the base of my dick, pulling it back up.

Within seconds, she was sucking me like a porn star, moaning all around my pipe.

I wrapped my fingers into her hair and went along with the bobbing of her head. I clenched my jaw as I slowly stroked in and out of her mouth. "Suck that dick, baby girl. Get it for daddy. Get it, ma."

She growled and increased her sucking speed. She stroked my dick up and down, slobbering all over it. She pulled it out of her mouth and smack it against her tongue, then inhaled me all over again. I reached under and played with her titties. The sight of them was doing something to me.

Her fists slid up and down my dick in a blur. She sucked on my head and ran her tongue up and down my pee hole before sucking at it. The heat was intense. Her mouth was wet. I grabbed her head with two hands, right on the sides like she'd did me and started to long stroke her mouth as my eyes rolled to the back of my head. I felt a tingling feeling deep down inside my balls.

"Aww, shit. Kalani, here it come. Here it come!" I hollered and jerked my hips forward in short jabs, my seed spilling out of me. I felt my whole body tingling. She kept on sucking and pumping him up and down, milking me. She swallowed and moaned deep within her throat, before popping my dick out.

"There you go, Buck City style. Red Hook Houses stand up!" She hollered, repping the housing projects she'd been raised in alongside of my brother, Tristian. She frowned.

"Damn, yo' dick still hard. What you tryna say?" she said, giggling.

I tried to hump into her hand. I was hornier than ever now since I got that first nut up out of me. "Yo, you finna give me some of that box now, shorty. Word is bond."

She stood and pulled her skirt down. She got serious. "That ain't happenin', Showbiz. I told you I'm not about to get down on your brother like that." She reached in between her legs and pulled her panties over her pussy. "Come on, I'm serious this time. It's time for you to go."

She wiped sweat from her forehead and started toward the front door. "Got me in my nigga's house sucking his brother's dick. What type of shit is that?" She shook her head.

I pulled my pants up just enough for me to run after her ass. I crashed into her, wrapping my arms around her waist, stabbing her in the ass with my hard dick.

"Yo, I'm finna hit this shit. I'm not going nowhere until you give me some of this pussy. That's my word, Kalani." I tackled her to the carpet.

"No! Get off me! I'm not about to do this." She swung her arms wildly, her fists connecting with my jaw.

I grabbed her wrist and planted them to the floor. "Stop all this muhfucking fighting and give me some of this shit, baby girl." I got between her thighs and pulled her panties to the side aggressively. All I could think about was how her pussy was going to feel. How it was going to feel to sink deep into her hot wet hole. I didn't give a fuck if she told Tristian. I needed more of her in the worst way.

"Please, get off me, Showbiz. We can't do this." She kicked her legs and tried to buck me off of her.

I wasn't about to let that happen. I was feening for that pussy. I needed to know what it felt like. I wanted it so bad that I was shaking as if it was freezing cold in that room. The excitement of taking pussy from a bad bitch, hyped me up even more.

I grabbed her between her sex lips and bucked forward, sliding deep into her channel. I felt like I was the first to run through the tape in a marathon that had a million runners.

She turned her head to the side and opened her mouth. "Aww! Fuck, Showbiz." She pushed at my chest weakly and opened her legs wider.

I got to jack hammering that pussy with force. I'd pulled my dick all the way back and slammed it home, then repeated the process. She was tight and wet, barely able to accommodate my size. Her walls squeezed at me.

"Uh! Uh! Give me this pussy. Give it to me. Give it to me, baby girl! I'm daddy now! You. Hear. Me!" I bit into her neck and got to fucking her as hard as I could while she held her leg on my shoulder.

"Aww! Aww! Showbiz! Showbiz! Shit, take this pussy! Aww shit, daddy!" she cried. She ran her hands under my shirt and dug her nails into my chest, rubbing all over my stomach muscles. "You daddy now. Harder! Fuck me harder!" she threw he head back and screamed, cumming all over my dick.

I sucked all over her brown nipples, my pole slicing her brown lips. Her hole juiced up and spilled over. Her essence poured out of her and onto the carpet.

"Anytime, anytime I want this pussy, you gon' give it to me! Word is bond. You hear me?" I flipped her on to her stomach and pushed her left leg to her ribs, before sliding back in and murdering that ass while I sank my teeth into the back of her neck. I smacked that big ass booty and squeezed it.

She was breathing hard. Moaning at the top of her lungs. "I don't believe this. I can't. Aww, fuck. Believe this. This is so wrong. It's so wrong. Shit! I'm cummin'." She came all over my pipe.

I plunged deeper and deeper. Sucked on her neck out of breath. I felt that feeling in my balls tingling all over.

Bam! Bam! Bam! Bam!

My dick worked in and out of her twat. I couldn't take it any longer. I needed to cum. Her pussy sucked at me righteously. I laid my cheek against hers, coming deep in her pussy, stroking in and out or her cat.

"Umm. Umm. Umm, Kalani. Umm, shit." I sucked all over her neck and slowly pulled out. My dick was dripping with her juices.

She turned on her side, getting into the fetal position. "You're so wrong, Showbiz. I never even thought you looked at me like that. How am I going to face Tristian after what we did?" she asked, refusing to look at me.

I slid behind her, dropping my face right on her cheeks. I spread them open, licking up and down her ass crack. Sucked on the anus and wiggled my tongue into her ass hole ."You just act like this never happened. Ain't nobody got to know about what we do. You can be my side dish and I'll be yours. You feel me?" I continued my work on her ass.

"Umm. Umm. Damn! How much fuckin' you tryna do? I'm tired. I don't feel good about myself right now." She arched her back, sucking on her bottom lip.

I wiped my mouth, slid behind her, hugging her to my chest. "Yo, it's good, baby. Why you stressing about the small shit? You don't think my brother slaying a Mexican bitch out in Cancun right now?" I rubbed my cheek against hers.

"I don't care if he is. Me and him ain't made no pact about being a hundred percent faithful to another. I know he's going to fuck something. But he ain't fucking my sister though." She sat up and looked back at me. "Then it's fucked up cuz you got some good dick, Showbiz. But I know if your brother find out, he would never marry me. And one day I look forward to him being my husband. I really do care about that man with all of my heart. I can't believe I slipped like this." Her eyes got watery.

I started to feel some type of way because I didn't mean to hurt her or nothing like that. I just wanted to see what that box was like, and now that I had, I was starting question if it was worth it. I pulled her up and into my warm embrace, looking into her brown eyes.

"Kalani, I can't really say I'm sorry because I wanted you so bad, but I didn't mean to hurt you. I got a lot of love and respect for you, but at the same time, I've been lusting after you for years. I know you crazy about my brother. You ain't never gotta worry about me sayin' shit. I got you." I hugged her and held her for a minute.

"Showbiz, I hope you ain't one of them thot ass Brooklyn niggas. Had you been any other nigga, I would have fought you 'til the death, but on some real shit, I've been kinda feelin' you, too. Not so much that I would have came at you though. That rough and tough shit you got goin' on intrigues me. You one of them crazy Harlem niggas, whereas your brother is more reserved and laid back. I grew up around animals like you, but never fucked with any of them. Just do me a favor, don't think any less of me. I'm already mentally goin' through some shit over this." She released a deep sigh.

"Shorty, you good. It's my fault, not yours. Don't blame yourself at all, a'ight? I just had to have you and that's what I got. Blame it on big bruh, it's good." I kissed her forehead and continued to hold her.

After a few minutes, she finally gave in and hugged me back. "Thanks, Showbiz. I appreciate that, but I think you and I both know what it is."

T.J. Edwards

Chapter 15

I spent the next three days making my rounds throughout Harlem. I felt like I was being bounced around like a ping pong ball machine. I was raking in bags of money every single day and placing orders with uncle Javier down in Havana. It was getting to the point that he had shipments of two hundred kilos at a time, coming up three times a week. And I still needed more.

Wetto had Spanish Harlem rocking. Even though he wasn't a killer, he was a pure business man. He'd found a way to penetrate the circles of the Crips and other rival gangs of Spanish Harlem and become their plugs. Since he was their plug and I was his, that meant that every hood he conquered, I conquered.

I was seeing five million a week easily. That money was used to cop a bigger shipment from my uncle Javier, which I in turn, dropped the whole package to Wetto and he'd do his thing. The money was coming fast and often.

Tori was still going to school trying to get one degree after the next so it could be used in the legal business community. All of the properties Eve ran before she passed away, Tori was now over them with me as her overseer.

She took her position extremely seriously. I watched her transform each mediocre business into classy enterprises. I was proud of her and loved watching her do her thing. I felt investing in her and her education had been one of the smartest things I'd ever done. I knew if the drug game ever took a turn for the worst, I could always fall back on our legal side of the coin.

My mother summoned me to her home about a week after me and Kalani had gotten down. It was a hot day in the city, about eighty degrees and it humid as hell. I jogged up the steps to her two story bricked home and before I could ring the doorbell, the door flew open. She had a worried expression on her face. "Baby come in, I need to speak with you."

She grabbed my wrist and pulled me inside of her place. She had on sheer robe. I could clearly make out her nudity. I turned my head in the opposite direction. "Ma, can you please put some clothes on? I can see everything."

She ignored me and grabbed my face with both hands. "Baby, your father is sick. He's going to die soon." She searched my eyes for a response.

Honestly, I felt nothing. Not one thing. No sadness. No fear. Not a damn thing. I didn't care. I'd proven to my father and myself, that I didn't need him to make it out of New York. As long as Uncle Javier and Wetto doing all my dirty work, I was good to go. I shrugged my shoulders. "That's unfortunate, ma, but what do you want me to do about it?" I looked into her eyes.

She smiled weakly. "Baby, he's dying because of me." She dropped her head and walked about 20 feet away from me before stopping in place. She sighed, running her fingers through her long, flowing hair.

"What are you talking about? Why is it your fault? What have you done?" I asked, walking toward her.

"Poisoning him, son. He would come by here every Sunday to pick up a plate of food. And before he'd get the food, we'd have relations. I've been putting small traces of rat poisoning into his food over the span of two months. Not enough to instantly kill him, but enough for his body to slowly begin to deteriorate. It's an old remedy us scorned women used back in Havana for our cheating husbands.

I scrunched my face. "But why, ma? Why would you do such a thing? I thought you still loved my father? You say it all the time." I was so confused. I felt like I needed a gram of dope to get my mind right.

"I did it for you, son. Now that your father has completely taken over the Vega fields, his riches are about to sky rocket. He's going to be making deals with powerful people all over world. His hand will extend across the country and back to our native land. I need for him to make all those connections. To get the Vega family in a prestigious position, only to step down and surrender his power over to you. Once that happens, we can live the dream, son. The dream that I've always had as a starving little girl growing up working in the sugar cane fields." She smiled, she was in a daze as if she had mentally gone to another place.

"Yo, I don't need my father to take us to the next level. I can make that happen on my own. I'm making stupid cash right now. And you can have as much of it as you want. You're my heart, you already know that."

"Money is nothing more than paper if you don't know what to do with it. You'll spend it, but no power will come from it if you do not have the right connections. You are the head of an entire generation and you don't even know it. It's about more than me, you, money and all that other bullshit. It's about legacy, son. Your legacy. You were meant to be great. It's my job as your mother to help you realize your potential. So man up!"

I scoffed, "Ma, I hear what you saying, but I don't care about nobody outside of you and I. Maybe my son and Tori, but that's it. My father been snubbing me my whole life, catering to Tristian's ass. As far as I'm concerned, he can give that hand-me-down shit to him. I'm good."

My phone buzzed and I saw Tristian's number come across the screen with a text saying he was ready for me to scoop him from the airport. "Speaking of the devil, this Tristian hitting me up right now. I promised I'd pick him up from JFK, so I gotta get a move on."

My mother blocked my path and grabbed my shirt with her small fists. "Don't you do this to me. Don't you let that bitch's son get what you're supposed to have. You're his first born. Everything that he accrued belongs to you first and foremost. You're supposed to be king of the Vegas after your father dies. I'm doing my part, so you must do yours. That's an order, Juanito!" she yelled.

I could see my mother's eyes getting watery and that hurt my heart. Her chest heaved up and down as she flared her nostrils. I could see how passionate she was. " A'ight, Ma. I'll do whatever you want me to do because I love you. And you're my everything. You've always had my back. If you want me to take over his throne and be what you've always wanted me to be, then I will." I removed her fists from my shirt, kissed her on the forehead and hugged her.

"You're supposed to be the great one, son. Nobody can steal your birthright. In Cuba, that offense is punishable by death. You must kill for what is yours. I will do my part. I promise you that."

* * *

I dropped the top on my Porsche so I could feel the breeze flowing through the city. Airplanes took flight off the runway a short distance from me, while others landed after their long journey. It was so loud that I couldn't understand how my son slept in the backseat so soundly. He'd been getting on my nerves whining and shit the entire time after I'd picked him up from Tori. I honestly didn't want to bring him along with me to begin with, but Tristian insisted on seeing his nephew, so here we were.

I let my seat back a bit and turned up the radio's volume, bumping the J. Cole album out of my speakers. Tristian strolled out of the doors of the airport with his luggage in tow. We made eye contact briefly before he made his way to the car, loading in his bags.

"Yo, so this how you doin' shit now?" he asked, tossing his things into the back seat beside Maine, taking a full glace of my whip.

"Nigga, I told you I wasn't copping any of these until I had a substantial amount of paper."

He opened the door and adjusted his seat before leaning over the console and shaking up with me.

"Yo, fuck that, Dunn. Leave the kid alone. His ass been driving me crazy all day long. He'll be up soon and y'all can shoot the shit then. Word up." I placed my whip in the first gear, pulling away from the airport. "So, how was Spring Break? You fuck a lot of foreign bitches down there?" I asked, thinking about how it looked with my dick going in and out of Kalani's tight pink pussy.

I couldn't help but think about the way she scratched my back up and moaned loudly in my ear. I could still feel her kisses all over my neck.

He shook his head. " I fucked a few, but for the most part, that trip was boring as hell. Them Cartel jokers down there was kidnapping tourists and demanding ransoms. If they didn't get their scratch, they was cutting heads off and tossing their dead bodies on the side of the roads. That shit was known for happening right in the area I was in.

Rather than me being able to enjoy myself the entire time, I had to stay on point and make sure I wasn't being set up by the lil' hoes I was fuckin' off wit'. It was crazy." He shook his head in disbelief, the sun hitting his deep waves. He pulled down the sun visor and squinted his eyes. "Kalani told me you checked on her too for me. I appreciate that. You know how crazy Brooklyn can get."

A slight smile crept across my face. I knew for a fact I'd be hitting shorty on a regular. I didn't care if I had to take the pussy every time. It was that good. And the way she fought me off every time was hot as hell.

"Yeah, don't mention it, kid. When I was over there, a crazy ass brawl broke out. I think your whole block was warring with one another, even the senior citizens. No bullshit." I laughed and stepped on the gas. I weaved in and out of traffic, speeding past car after car on the highway. Tristan sat his forearm on the windowsill and nodded his head to the J. Cole track.

"You think J. Cole better than Jay?"

"Nall, kid. He hot, but Jay is a fucking legend. On top of that, he's a Brooklyn nigga like you, so there is no question about who's hotter."

"Yeah, you were right. Neither one of them niggas fucking with Big though. Kid still got the Apple and the world at large on lock. Word is bond." Tristian nodded his head.

"No doubt about that. Pac was never on Big's level. I don't give a fuck what nobody say."

"Yo turn that bass up a lil' bit and lemme hear you spit one of them Harlem freestyles. Welcome back to the land, son. Gon' head, word up," he encouraged me.

I left, adjusting the base like he had asked me. I didn't feel like spitting, but thought why not. I knew one in my head, so I got a beat.

"A'ight, you can catch me in a Porsche the color of cherrywood, bad bitch in my lap, sucking the wood. Don't usually don't like to start, I stick them jerks. I carry a .45 like bitches carry a purse. The kids berserk, ain't smashing out less than a dollar. Twenty-eight grams a run you eight, a ball ain't less than a dollar. Plus, I keep a Cola that's classic. A now and later Jag, disrespectful in traffic.

Jellybean interior. My name in the head rest. Smart screen Panoramic's, thirty-eight where the legs at. I'm chosen, first pick making the draft. I keep snow with birds like Don McNabb. In big pots, we whip whops and shovel the cane. Fiends lined up like Six Flags and patient for the grains. I am popping kilos for thirteen flooding the block. It's Harlem's world, Showbiz got the game on lock." I laughed as we dapped each other up.

"Nigga, that shit crazy. You still got skills like that off the top of the dome." He looked back over his shoulder at Maine. "Yo, I wanna take him on vacation with me in a few weeks, too. Whatchu think about that?"

I shrugged my shoulders. "I don't give a fuck. It's cool with me. I just gotta run that shit by Tori. You know how overprotective she is over shorty. She be acting like she spit him out and shit ever since Punkin' died." My face frowned as I turned onto West on 155th Street.

I looked in the parking lot and saw Flex's bitch ass knelt down along side a Cadillac Escalade, shining one of the big rims on the truck. I felt my heart starting to pump harder in my chest. I took my .45 from underneath the seat and set it on my lap, pulling into the parking lot a few spaces away from him and his crew.

Flex was a cutthroat Harlem nigga that lived in both, Spanish Harlem and out in Brooklyn. When I was just a young teenager, he and I used to hit licks together whenever I wasn't hitting them with Eve.

About four months back, I had fronted him three breaks of heroin and told him to hit me back with a hundred and fifty thousand once he got right. Well, after getting the product, he never hit my phone and I hadn't heard from him since then until this day.

I didn't give a fuck how much money I had or how quickly it came. I wasn't about to let no nigga get over on me. I had visions of knocking son's shit out of his head right there in that parking lot. I didn't give a fuck if there were a bunch of kids playing on the playground. I was a Harlem nigga and bound to be king of the Vegas. I had to set the precedent right then and there.

I cocked the .45 and slid it into the waistband of my Burberry's, opening the door to my Porsche.

"Yo, you finna do that shit wit Maine in the car?" Tristan asked, looking around nervously.

"Yo, grab that foe nickel out of my glove box and make sure these niggas don't slap me if it comes down to it. Son got all my money. I gotta have mine." I threw open the door and slammed it. Made my way across the parking lot, feeling the gravel under my space jam Jordans that matched my Burberry fit.

The wind blew into my face, causing me to squint my eyes. There was no shade anywhere around, so the sun was beaming on me like an interrogation light. I could smell the chemical of the spray he was using to buff his rooms. The sounds of the children playing in the playground behind me was loud in my ears.

"Yo, what's good, kid? Long time no hear from.? I hollered, walking up to his kneeling form, clenching my jaw.

Flex must have heard my voice, because he jumped up and dropped a bottle of armor all on the ground and held two hands out in front of him. "Aww shit, damn. Yo, I know I ain't got up with you, Show-biz, but I just been on some other shit. I should have that bread for you in a few weeks. I mean you know how it is out here."

I shook my head." Nall, nigga, fuck that. It's been more than three months. You gon' give me my shit right now." I upped my .45 and smacked him across the face with it, splitting his shit.

He fell to one knee and held his face. "Fuck! Man, shoot this bitch ass nigga! What the fuck y'all waitin' on?" Flex hollered.

Two of the niggas that were standing outside of the trucks with him opened the doors to the Escalade and reached inside of them. I saw one of them come up with a nickel plated Mach. He cocked it, slamming the door back. My eyes got as big as paper plates. I aimed at him and pull the trigger just as his man's begin to unload his pistol in my direction.

To be continued...
King of New York 4
Coming Soon

Submission Guideline

Submit the first three chapters of your completed manuscript to ldpsubmissions@gmail.com, subject line: Your book's title. The manuscript must be in a .doc file and sent as an attachment. Document should be in Times New Roman, double spaced and in size 12 font. Also, provide your synopsis and full contact information. If sending multiple submissions, they must each be in a separate email.

Have a story but no way to send it electronically? You can still submit to LDP/Ca$h Presents. Send in the first three chapters, written or typed, of your completed manuscript to:

LDP: Submissions Dept
Po Box 870494
Mesquite, Tx 75187

DO NOT send original manuscript. Must be a duplicate.

Provide your synopsis and a cover letter containing your full contact information.

Thanks for considering LDP and Ca$h Presents.

Coming Soon from Lock Down Publications/Ca$h Presents

BOW DOWN TO MY GANGSTA

By **Ca$h**

TORN BETWEEN TWO

By **Coffee**

BLOOD STAINS OF A SHOTTA **III**

By **Jamaica**

STEADY MOBBIN **III**

By **Marcellus Allen**

BLOOD OF A BOSS **V**

By **Askari**

LOYAL TO THE GAME **IV**

LIFE OF SIN II

By **T.J. & Jelissa**

A DOPEBOY'S PRAYER **II**

By **Eddie "Wolf" Lee**

IF LOVING YOU IS WRONG… **III**

LOVE ME EVEN WHEN IT HURTS **II**

By **Jelissa**

TRUE SAVAGE **VI**

By **Chris Green**

BLAST FOR ME **III**

A BRONX TALE III

DUFFLE BAG CARTEL

By **Ghost**

ADDICTIED TO THE DRAMA **III**

By **Jamila Mathis**

LIPSTICK KILLAH **III**

WHAT BAD BITCHES DO **III**

KILL ZONE **II**

By **Aryanna**

THE COST OF LOYALTY **II**

By **Kweli**

SHE FELL IN LOVE WITH A REAL ONE **II**

By **Tamara Butler**

LOVE SHOULDN'T HURT **III**

RENEGADE BOYS **III**

By **Meesha**

CORRUPTED BY A GANGSTA **IV**

By **Destiny Skai**

A GANGSTER'S CODE **III**

By **J-Blunt**

KING OF NEW YORK IV

By **T.J. Edwards**

GORILLAS IN THE BAY II

De'Kari

THE STREETS ARE CALLING II

Duquie Wilson

KINGPIN KILLAZ III

Hood Rich

STEADY MOBBIN' **III**

Marcellus Allen

SINS OF A HUSTLA II

ASAD

HER MAN, MINE'S TOO **II**

CASH MONEY HOES

Nicole Goosby

TRIGGADALE II

Elijah R. Freeman

Available Now

RESTRAINING ORDER **I & II**

By **CA$H & Coffee**

LOVE KNOWS NO BOUNDARIES **I II & III**

By **Coffee**

RAISED AS A GOON I, II, III & IV

BRED BY THE SLUMS I, II, III

BLAST FOR ME I & II

ROTTEN TO THE CORE I III

A BRONX TALE I, II

By **Ghost**

LAY IT DOWN **I & II**

LAST OF A DYING BREED

BLOOD STAINS OF A SHOTTA I & II

By **Jamaica**

LOYAL TO THE GAME

LOYAL TO THE GAME II

LOYAL TO THE GAME III

LIFE OF SIN

By **TJ & Jelissa**

BLOODY COMMAS I & II

SKI MASK CARTEL I II & III

KING OF NEW YORK I II,III

By **T.J. Edwards**

IF LOVING HIM IS WRONG…I & II

LOVE ME EVEN WHEN IT HURTS

By **Jelissa**

WHEN THE STREETS CLAP BACK I & II III

By **Jibril Williams**

A DISTINGUISHED THUG STOLE MY HEART I II & III

LOVE SHOULDN'T HURT I II

RENEGADE BOYS I & II

By **Meesha**

A GANGSTER'S CODE I & II

By J-Blunt

PUSH IT TO THE LIMIT

By **Bre' Hayes**

BLOOD OF A BOSS **I, II, III & IV**

By **Askari**

THE STREETS BLEED MURDER **I, II & III**

THE HEART OF A GANGSTA I II& III

By **Jerry Jackson**

CUM FOR ME

CUM FOR ME 2

CUM FOR ME 3

CUM FOR ME 4

T.J. Edwards

By **Chris Green**

A DOPEBOY'S PRAYER

By **Eddie "Wolf" Lee**

THE KING CARTEL **I, II & III**

By **Frank Gresham**

THESE NIGGAS AIN'T LOYAL **I, II & III**

By **Nikki Tee**

GANGSTA SHYT **I II &III**

By **CATO**

THE ULTIMATE BETRAYAL

By **Phoenix**

BOSS'N UP **I , II & III**

By **Royal Nicole**

I LOVE YOU TO DEATH

By Destiny J

I RIDE FOR MY HITTA

I STILL RIDE FOR MY HITTA

By **Misty Holt**

LOVE & CHASIN' PAPER

By **Qay Crockett**

TO DIE IN VAIN

SINS OF A HUSTLA

By **ASAD**

BROOKLYN HUSTLAZ

By **Boogsy Morina**

BROOKLYN ON LOCK I & II

By **Sonovia**

T.J. Edwards

GANGSTA CITY

By **Teddy Duke**

A DRUG KING AND HIS DIAMOND I & II III

A DOPEMAN'S RICHES

HER MAN, MINE'S TOO

By Nicole Goosby

TRAPHOUSE KING **I II & III**

KINGPIN KILLAZ

By **Hood Rich**

LIPSTICK KILLAH **I, II**

CRIME OF PASSION I & II

By **Mimi**

STEADY MOBBN' **I, II**

By **Marcellus Allen**

WHO SHOT YA **I, II**

Renta

GORILLAZ IN THE BAY

DE'KARI

TRIGGADALE

Elijah R. Freeman

GOD BLESS THE TRAPPERS I, II, III

THESE SCANDALOUS STREETS I, II, III

FEAR MY GANGSTA I, II, III

THESE STREETS DON'T LOVE NOBODY I, II

Tranay Adams

THE STREETS ARE CALLING

Duquie Wilson

186

BOOKS BY LDP'S CEO, CA$H

TRUST IN NO MAN

TRUST IN NO MAN 2

TRUST IN NO MAN 3

BONDED BY BLOOD

SHORTY GOT A THUG

THUGS CRY

THUGS CRY 2

THUGS CRY 3

TRUST NO BITCH

TRUST NO BITCH 2

TRUST NO BITCH 3

TIL MY CASKET DROPS

RESTRAINING ORDER

RESTRAINING ORDER 2

IN LOVE WITH A CONVICT

Coming Soon

BONDED BY BLOOD 2

BOW DOWN TO MY GANGSTA

T.J. Edwards